The Case of the Filthy Beast

by

Emily Karmazin

Cover Art by *The Wild Rose Press, Inc.*

The Wild Rose Press, Inc.
PO Box 708
Adams Basin, NY 14410-0708
Visit us at www.thewildrosepress.com

Publishing History
First Edition, 2024
Trade Paperback ISBN 978-1-5092-5678-5
Digital ISBN 978-1-5092-5679-2

Published in the United States of America

Chapter One

I took a bite of my ham and cheese sandwich and chewed. As a staff nurse on an inpatient floor in a small community hospital, getting off my feet for a break was a highlight of any day. Eating, a close second. The blue light mounted on the wall above my head blinked on and off; then, the pager at my hip chirped as the operator made the announcement over the intercom. *Code blue... emergency room two.*

I dropped my sandwich, ran for the stairs and literally flew down the treaded carpet, hoping I didn't fall flat on my ass in the process.

Atherton Hospital's ER has only five beds and those are rarely full but because we serve a population of several thousand in the contiguous counties, it's important to maintain a presence even if we're small. The stair well door banged open as I flew to bed two carried on the sounds of machines going crazy.

A paramedic, shell-shocked in his eyes grabbed my scrub top as I passed. "We tried to stop the bleeding. We did. There was so much."

I cursed to myself. Mike Griffin, the local certified public accountant, had no business volunteering as an EMT just because he'd been a medic in the army in the last century. But in small town Atherton, everyone pitched in wherever they could. I shrugged him off, dodged machinery and staff to the bedside.

"I've got a pulse, barely. Sara, make sure the airway stays clear." Kavitha Kumar, the emergency room physician, stood calm and focused as she directed other staff while continuing chest compressions.

"Lex, we've got to stop the bleeding," she shouted at me. "Her pressure is too low. Let's do suppressors; increase the fluids. Someone get five units of O positive blood in here."

Standing at the foot of the bed, I popped on medical gloves, grabbed a wad of gauze, and went to work. The patient's leg was painfully small and cold to the touch. Fresh blood flowed from mangled flesh. There were so many wounds; it was impossible to tell where one slash began and the next ended. Long blonde hair flecked with blood spread spread out over the pillow. A girl, no older than twelve, lay beneath all that blood and gore.

A nurse standing next to me worked on the patient's midsection. Again, there were so many wounds. "What the hell happened?" she muttered to me. "No traffic accident causes injuries like this."

I continued wiping the blood away as best as possible and applied pressure to the leg wounds. Cleaning and suturing would happen once they got the patient to the nearest trauma center in Kansas City. It was our job to stabilize her for transport. Saving her life wouldn't be quick or easy, but any recovery would be better than the odds the patient had right now.

As the disturbing constant beep of the flat line on the EKG machine echoed throughout the room.

Kavitha stepped back from the patient, breathless from the exhaustion common after a resuscitation. "There's nothing more we can do." She glanced up at the clock on the wall. "Time of death, eighteen hundred hours and fourteen minutes."

We stepped away from the slight body and collectively exhaled. Someone pulled a bloodstained sheet over the remains. A quiet settled as we cleaned the gauze and IV bags and other supplies strewn across the room. I turned to leave and noticed a strand of blood-stained hair had slipped out from under the sheet. My chest tightened. I tucked it back in. A mother shouldn't see that.

I tugged the gloves off and dragged the curtain closed in the room then and turned to the hand washing station. The paramedic still stood in the hallway. I rested a hand on his shoulder. "You did everything possible."

Mike stared straight ahead, not acknowledging me. I squeezed his shoulder and gave him a shake. He blinked and his chest rose on a rough inhale. "How about we get you a snack and a drink?"

He nodded his head and turned, robotic towards the lounge. "My granddaughter, she's..." He glanced around the emergency room with a stare that said he didn't remember how he got here. "She's a little girl, too."

The trained professional on the EMS team stepped up and wrapped an arm around him, ushering Mike inside. The ER had a small lounge for paramedics. It was only the size of a large closet, but it would give him a place to recover. I watched Mike for a moment, unable to imagine the scene they had rolled up on.

Kavitha vigorously scrubbed her hands at the sink. Strands of dark, curly hair hung limp around her face. I tore off the paper gown and joined her, welcoming the strong antiseptic soap scent that cut through the coppery odor of blood. Still, I knew I would smell it for days.

I bumped shoulders with Kavitha. "We did everything conceivable."

She didn't look up but kept scrubbing. "It's never enough." Her voice wavered.

"What happened?" It didn't matter how many code blues I worked, they were all hard, but one with a kid was especially tough.

Kavitha shook her head. "The call said an animal attack. She simply lost too much blood."

I nodded. Blood was the life force. If a body lost too much, the organs slowly shut down, one by one, essentially starved. "It looked like something mauled her."

She dried her hands and sighed heavily, looking older than her forty years. "She was as good as dead when they rolled her in. Did you see the abdomen? It looked like something had ripped it open. What does that mean? We haven't had a dog bite or attack in I don't know how long."

Atherton was what us lifelong residents referred to as the county. Not quite country, not quite city. A city planner I dated years ago jokingly referred to it as a bedroom community. We were close enough to the woods and open plains to have the occasional wildlife animal wander in. Feral dogs and cats were common, as was the occasional fox and racoon that wandered into populated areas in search of food.

I had been at the hospital since I graduated from nursing school in the city, almost twenty years ago. Some of those years were in the emergency room. "Remember that one drunk guy from a couple years back who tried to befriend that racoon?" Kavitha nodded. "Can't say I remember one in the last few years," I said.

"But never one this bad."

"I don't think I have either," she said. "Ever. I'll do the exam for the coroner."

The coroner for Sibley County is an elected position. It wasn't uncommon for the coroner to have little to no medical experience. The current one was a physician but one of the laziest known to humankind and often expected the ER docs to prepare the report he which he then signed off on.

"How long have you been on?" Physicians and nurses were worth their weight in gold and worked long shifts since there were never enough of them. Kavitha was worth twice her slight weight.

"Too long." She closed her eyes and scrunched her eyebrows together. She sighed again and shook her head. "They keep saying they're hiring new staff, but I never see them, just more hours and shiny brochures."

"Want me to get you some coffee? A snack?" I dried my hands and resisted the urge to wrap an arm around her shoulders. The loss of a patient affected people. I wasn't one to cater to physicians, but we were friends.

"No thanks, I've got a big one at my desk. I'll chug it and get back." She looked at her watch. "Only two hours left and then I have a bubble bath calling my name."

"You still up for girl's night?" I attempted a happier tone, but it fell flat. I didn't have it in me. The hospital was small and a few of us got together now and then. This month was a painting and wine tasting class.

Kavitha favored me with a small smile. "Wine and painting random landscapes? How can I pass that up? It sounds better than sitting on the couch watching a Netflix marathon."

"You will have to wear pants, though." This time, my laughter was genuine. It didn't matter how many hours Kavitha worked, she always looked professional and pulled together at work. But if you caught her at home, she wore an oversized top, boy shorts, and tied her hair up in a messy bun.

She twisted her mouth. "No one told me pants were required, but I guess I can put some on."

"All right, see you then. Take care." I patted her on the shoulder and trudged up the stairs to my unit. My feet dragged with each step. The entire code had lasted less than thirty minutes, but it seemed like an eternity. It didn't matter how long they lasted, they always took a physical and mental toll on me.

Upstairs, I dropped into the chair and tried to finish my sandwich. It turned into a ball of paste in my mouth. The crunch of the side of chips was a welcomed change in texture, but the bag was empty too soon. I threw it in the trash and scrunched my face when another nurse walked in. I didn't want to tell talk about the code.

Tracey Phillips crossed her arms and leaned against the door frame. "So, what happened?"

I shook my head. "Code on an animal attack. Too much blood loss before the rig even rolled in. She didn't have much of a chance." If I kept saying it, I might convince myself.

"Animal attack? Here in Atherton?" She shook her head incredulously. "When was the last time we had an animal attack here? I can't even remember."

"Neither can I, nor Kavitha." I shrugged. "I don't know." My voice trailed off. The image of the pale leg and scarlet streaked hair filled my mind, and my vision blurred. I grabbed a napkin and wiped my face.

"I understood there's some stray dog packs on the outskirts of town. People drop the poor mutts out to fend for themselves." Tracey's eyebrows attempted to scrunch together, but her latest Botox injection kept it from happening.

I slumped in the chair. Exhaustion weighed on my shoulders. My stomach churned. "That's an old urban legend. My dad used to tell us that to keep us out of the woods by the river."

Tracey nodded. "Well, whatever it was, I'm sorry you all had to go through that. Why don't you go on home? Mindy got here early."

Of course, Mindy Michaels clocked in early. Fresh out of nursing school, she wanted to make a good impression. Normally, I'd finish my shift. But the blonde hair streaming over the pillow burned in my mind. I put up a bit of a protest to be a good employee. Tracey and I exchanged a few more words before she gave me a warm hug and sent me home. I grabbed my oversized tote and threw it over my shoulder. It carried my life and half of my friend Zelda's in it. I pulled my phone out and texted her.

—Just had a code. Rough one —

At the elevator, the usual post-code second guessing took over. Had we done everything possible to save her? What if we had lowered her body temp and then tried to stop the bleeding from the wounds, would she have survived?

I shook my head and fidgeted with the trim on the tote handle. If she had survived, she would have had debilitating scars and needed years of cosmetic surgeries and physical therapy in order to walk again. No, we did all we imaginably could. As much as I hated to admit it, the kid was as good as dead when she was rolled in. My phone dinged with a notification. Zelda.

—I'm sorry, girl. Is there anything I can do to help?—

—Eh? I don't think so. It was an awful scene, lots of blood, younger kid.—

Zelda replied.

—Shit. I can't imagine it's ever easy, but a kid has to be one of the worst. Take a walk and clear your head? I'm teaching tonight, but I'll light a candle for you. XOXO—

A walk might be a good idea to clear my head. But I wasn't sure I had the energy. I plodded across the parking garage, my car seemed to be miles away. My legs were filled with cement and my feet ached. My smart watch dinged a text notification from my boyfriend Scott Devlin.

—Heard about the animal attack. Stop by later, got a pot of chili going.—

Of course, he heard. My boyfriend was one of two detectives on the Atherton Police force. He made great chili, but I wasn't sure I wanted to be around other people right now. My emotions were all over the place and my body was exhausted. But being alone sounded worse.

I clicked the thumbs up button in response and got in the car. I rested my arms on the steering wheel and dropped my head. Tears flowed. For how long I didn't know. When it stopped, I wiped a hand across my face and sighed. If a code affected me this much, perhaps it was time for me to get out of nursing.

No, something else bothered me about it. What I couldn't put my finger on yet. I checked the back seat to make sure I had a clean change of clothes and started the car. On the way to Scott's, I turned up the radio and blared 1980's hair metal band. The songs pushed everything out of my mind.

The spices and richness of chili might be just enough to drive the scent of blood out of my nose.

Chapter Two

I parked my car in front of Scott's small ranch house and pulled my aching body out of the bucket seat. The cooling late fall air caused the fine hairs on my arms to stand up. At times like this, I debated about retiring from nursing. Teaching might be an option. Every passing year took a heavier toll on my body.

My phone dinged and I wearily glanced at the screen. A text from my mom.

–*Alexandra, your father just got a deal on a cruise to the Bahamas. You know we won't pay for Wi-Fi and probably won't have cell service so please talk to me before we leave.*–

Groaning, I knocked once and opened the door. The smell of chili engulfed me, and I moaned. Scott used his Grandma McCarty's blue-ribbon recipe, and it was better than most over- the-counter medications for what ailed you. After one bowl, I'd be snoring on the sofa. I was off for the next three days and could afford to lose consciousness for a while. Hell, I looked forward to the blackout.

"Hey, babe." Scott stood in the kitchen, a pan of cornbread muffins in his mittened hand. Some people ate cinnamon rolls with their chili. They were wrong. Cornbread was the only way. His gaze bore into me, and his auburn brows furrowed. "That bad, uh?"

I dropped my tote on the kitchen counter and

grabbed a bottle of beer from the refrigerator. "Yeah, something about the code... I can't shake it."

"Give it some time, it'll fade."

I nodded but didn't feel it as I headed to the bathroom. A few minutes later, showered and changed into yoga pants and a sweatshirt, I walked into the kitchen. He took bowls out of the cabinet and set them on the counter, filling them with ladles of thick goodness. "The animal mauling. I pulled the case."

In the four years we had dated, our paths hadn't crossed professionally. I'm a floor nurse and he usually handles property crimes and the occasional domestic situation. "I heard an animal was involved," I said around a mouthful of hot chili.

Scott broke up a couple of cornbread muffins and mixed the crumbs into the chili. "Yeah, looks that way." He took a bite.

I took a swig of beer. Answers might calm the rising anxiety in me. "Who found her?"

"You know Neveah Jenkins?" I nodded. "She was walking past Celeste Stewart's house. Said she saw the blood and wanted to see what was happening. Screamed. Celeste came out of the house, passed out. Neighbor called 911 over the commotions." He shoved another bite in and shrugged.

Neveah Jenkins was a young woman who most days would be seen with earphones on her head and an old portable CD player in her hand walking around town. She was a sweet kid, but not the smartest. My best friend, Zelda, had taught her in history and English class at the local high school and had struggled to get her to graduation. Neveah had a kind heart and always asked after people. I only imagined how the scene affected her.

She'd probably have nightmares for weeks.

I pushed my bowl away, no longer hungry. "So, she'd been laying on the side of the house for a while?" The idea of the little girl bleeding out in the dead leaves struck a chord in my heart. She had no chance. Might be I should leave this alone.

He shrugged between bites. "Not that long, probably. Neveah said she saw blood pumping out of the body and what she described as a large, hairy thing running away. But who knows? She's not the most reliable witness."

I slammed the beer bottle down, suds rising to the neck. "A what?"

Scott's eyebrows raised. "She said the thing was bigger than a dog, more like a dire wolf. Whatever the hell that is."

"It's an animal popular in fantasy stuff recently and believed to be extinct." It's amazing what one learns viewing documentaries as you fall asleep.

He shoveled another bite in unbothered. "They occasionally find animals they thought extinct, but I doubt that's the case here."

I agreed. "Anyone else see anything?"

He ran a hand across his dark auburn beard. "Not so far. I'll canvass more tomorrow. Celeste was inside, the afternoon talk shows on full volume. Can't imagine she heard much over the television blaring. Neighbor next door called 911 because of the screams."

"That's a busy path, right? Kids cut through the yard to the gas station?" On my walks and sometimes runs, I noticed kids cutting through Celeste's lawn.

"Yeah. The after-school crowd had already gone through. Deserted."

I crossed my arms against myself. "Poor Neveah. Was she okay?"

"As good as expected. I'll talk to her more tomorrow."

"Did you notify the family? Identify the body?"

"Flip those, but yes. The girl had her school ID on her, and Neveah recognized her. Buffy something or another. Kid, teenager that goes – went - to school with Neveah's younger brother. The Chief notified the family."

"Buffy something or another?"

His lackadaisical attitude drained my energy. I got that he was disengaged from the emotional aspect of the case. Perhaps I was too engaged. Heat rose in my face. This wasn't the time to lose my temper. My reaction might come from exhaustion and raging emotions. I didn't care. He didn't see many deaths.

With a shrug, Scott shrugged, scraped the spoon against the empty bowl. "Stephens? Doesn't matter. It was an animal mauling. I'll interview a few people, wrap up the paperwork, and file the report. On to the next one."

"So, the investigation is done?" Despite internal warnings, a note of anger rose in my voice.

He gave a small smile. "Mostly, yeah. She walked in the wrong place at the wrong time. Unfortunate, yes, but it happens. Animal Control will keep an eye out."

He dismissed the girl's life like it was a traffic ticket. "What type of animal will they keep an eye out for? Since you haven't investigated her death, how will they recognize what to watch for?"

"I don't know, Lex. The doctor will write the report, the coroner will sign off, and I'll close the case. End of story."

He got up from the table. I watched him fill his bowl again. A girl was dead, and he was getting seconds. His callousness left me speechless. After a moment, I found my voice. "Wait a minute, you don't even care about solving the crime? Finding out what happened?"

He shook his head. "C'mon, you know that's not true. I care about the crimes. And the victims I work with. Things are usually exactly what they seem to be. There's nothing to examine. There's nothing to investigate."

"There has to be more to it than that. Like caring about finding the truth?"

Scott slammed his bowl, drops of chili flew on the table. "Why does there have to be more than that? It's cut and dry, Lex. Just because you're getting emotional, because of whatever, it's not my fault."

I felt the blood rise in my cheeks. *"Because of whatever?* Just come out and say what you mean, Scott."

He held up his hands in defense. "Look, I'm just saying maybe you need to get out of direct care. With your age and meno–"

"Oh!" I shouted over him. "So glad you are at least concerned for my aged reproductive system and my damn emotions, but not for a murdered child."

"Damn it, Lexi. Be sensible here. What do you want me to do? Go arrest a German Sheppard and put the dog on trial? Walk Fido to the electric chair?"

How do you explain to someone they should care for another human being? "I don't feel certain I'm in the best place to have this conversation."

"Ha." A dry laugh escaped him. "Great. You're not the only one with emotions here."

One of the reasons my first marriage broke up in my twenties was I was the only one in it. I promised myself I wouldn't do that again. "Then act like it." I shook my head. "It's not just me. I can't carry the whole emotional side of this relationship."

I watched a flush spread from his neck to hairline "Look, no one asked you to carry the emotional load. In my line of work, I can't afford to be emotional. I can't turn my emotions on and off. It's not a switch. If you would just calm down, we can talk."

I didn't want to talk or spend the night. The warm comfort I usually found here had gone cold. I carried my dishes into the kitchen and sat them in the sink. "I'll be heading home."

He stood to follow me. "You're leaving? We're in the middle of talking about this."

I nodded. "Yeah, we've had this conversation enough times, Scott. Thanks for the dinner." I gave him a tight smile, grabbed my tote, and turned to the door.

"So, this is how you want this to end? Just like that?"

My heart was numb, whether from exhaustion or heartache, I didn't know. "Yeah, like that."

"Okay, well, take care of yourself." His tone carried the ending of our relationship.

The unsaid words between us filled the small, tidy ranch house. We had reached a point in our relationship when it was time for the next step–and marriage loomed between us. The years were coming faster and faster. I wasn't sure I wanted to move forward. Scott was a great guy, but it was clear our beliefs didn't align. And I didn't want the past to repeat itself.

At the door, we exchanged a dry kiss. As I drove away, I realized more than just a kid had died on my watch today.

Chapter Three

Over my days off, the hospital crowd escaped for the night to the paint and sip party. Kavitha wore pants; masterpieces were painted; a few cabs were called after too many sips. Overall, the night was a success. Between meal planning for work, cooking, and cleaning, I kept busy. The fact I was ignoring Scott barely crossed my mind.

When Zelda's notification tone sounded, I read the message.

—*Shit. So the code you got was an animal mauling, right?*—

I stared at the phone screen, hesitant. Zelda and I were like sisters, and I told her everything. But there were privacy laws, even in a small town.

—*Yeah–I stopped there and hit send.*—

Three dancing notes showed Zelda was typing.

—*She was one of mine.*—

I should have known. Zelda taught at the local high school and every kid in town passed through her class at one time or another. I responded.

—*Damn Zel. I'm sorry. I should have known and said something*—.

—*It's okay. I'm just never prepared, you know? Especially losing one like this*—.

I didn't have words to fix or even soothe the situation for her. Twenty years of teaching and she'd lost a handful of students. With current events, that was a feat but there was one thing that might help.

—*How about we go for happy hour soon?*—

The response dots started as soon as I hit send.

—*Yes, please! It's been too long!*—

I laughed out loud. Zelda and I grew up down the street from each other and hadn't gone more than a week without seeing each other—not counting college—throughout our lifetimes.

—*We just went...four days ago...but okay! And there's nothing a good margarita and fried foods wouldn't fix—*.

Nothing like spinach dip and fried, saucy shrimps to process grief.

****

Back at work, Buffy Stephens' death remained the talk of Atherton Community Hospital. I understood the interest, but the gossip only infuriated me. The 'talkers' hadn't been there and seen the degree of trauma. Her death appeared nothing more than fodder for their beady little minds.

"I heard a pit bull just tore her apart," a floater nurse I never worked with explained. "You know they're vicious."

"That's a load of crap. Any dog can be vicious. My aunt had a straight up evil Cocker Spaniel," Tracey muttered, and shook her head. "And if it was a dog attack, wouldn't there have been another? It can't just be running around town unseen."

I continued charting, but as my attention stayed on the conversation, heat rose to my cheeks and my leg bounced faster and faster.

"Could it be a mountain lion or something? A fox?"

the floater continued. "Some people have been seeing things over by the railroad tracks. You know that clump of woods near those old warehouses? My cousin was over there making a delivery and said he saw a big dog or something."

Tracey shook her head. "Foxes only attack if they're sick or being attacked, and wouldn't the mountain lion have been seen or something? I'm gonna go with a Cocker Spaniel."

The image of Buffy's bloody leg in my hand filled my mind. The skin had been torn, but I had seen no flesh missing. Wouldn't an animal have eaten some of it? Or at least torn chucks out? Kavitha's comment about the injuries to the abdomen came back to me. I finished the chart and closed the tab before opening the internet and pulling up animal bites.

Photos of dogs filled the page. I sniffed. Like dogs were the only animals to bite. In third grade, Sam Neary bit me on the hand because I wouldn't be his girlfriend. My hand still had a couple of faint, white spots on it.

"You were there? Right? On the code?" The floater chewed noisily on a mouthful of brownie. "Were the limbs still attached? What about the muscles? Were they torn up? I heard it was a bloodbath." Her voice held too much excitement for my liking.

I opened my mouth to speak, but Tracey interrupted. "Really? That's how you ask something like that? And that's the language you use?" The floater shrunk in her chair, her mouth a wide O of surprise but my savior Tracey wasn't done. "No, Lex isn't answering anything until you phrase those questions better. Work on your empathy for Chrissakes." She glanced at me. "Sorry, Lex."

"Thanks." I locked the workstation and stood. "I'm going down to the cafeteria. Want anything?" Eyes downcast, they shook their heads. I headed down the stairs.

Instead of the cafeteria, I detoured to the ER to check in on Kavitha. She should have more insight. Certainly, more than the gossip hounds.

I found her at a workstation in the back corner of the Emergency Room. The large monitor almost blocked her completely from view. "Hey, if I didn't know better, I would say you are hiding. How's it going?" I took a seat next to her.

Kavitha had a large coffee, water jug, and assorted fruit and nuts in front of her. "Pretty good. It's my first day back on rotation." She popped a handful of snacks in her mouth. "You're here about Buffy Stephens, aren't you?"

A smile broke out on my lips. "Is it that obvious?"

After she pushed the container of nuts and dried fruit toward me, and I took a handful. "It was a rough case." She shook her head. "It's been a while since I had seen anything like that. I thought when I left the city, I'd be leaving things traumas like that behind. The occasional messy car wreck or bar fight, sure, not what we saw."

"I'm still wondering where they got the name Buffy."

Kavitha nodded. "Her parents were a fan of the old vampire show." She shrugged. "It's cute either way and there are worse names.

I laughed and nodded. Most nurses had a list of names they would never give their children. First on my list was Mindy. "Did you do the autopsy?" I popped the snack mix in my mouth, the sweetness exploded.

She shook her head. "Nope, Sanji Nakamura did it. As is his right as the coroner and the Stephens' family physician. Said he felt a responsibility to the family." She rolled her eyes. Nakamura had been the town coroner for decades and possibly the oldest still practicing physician in the state. He might have been good at one time but was now famous for mixing up patients and declaring breathing people dead. Most of the town stayed away from him, but there were a few stalwarts that stood by him.

"Have you seen the report?" I asked and grabbed another handful.

"All one page of it?" she asked with a raised eyebrow. "Yeah, I did. He didn't even try to say whether the bites were human or animal or even measure them. I don't know how he still keeps a practice running." She wiped her hands together in dismissal. "He needs to retire."

"So, all the gossip is just that. No one knows anything for sure. But not specifically what animal?"

Kavitha nodded and chugged the water.

"And no one is questioning anything?" If it had been my kid, I would tear Nakamura and the town apart for answers.

"You got it. Of course, it's insane." Kavitha's voice rose an octave in the last word. She tucked a stray curl behind her ear. "If Nakamura had just been thorough, it would stop half the stories floating around. The town has seen nothing like this in years." She rolled her eyes again. "Go on, ask me if he cares."

"You didn't want to get involved? Help clear things up?"

She shook her head. "I would have liked to, but I've

done my good karma for the week and honestly, I don't have time to do everything. My schedule here as primary ER physician and occasional surgeon keeps me busy, as my mother likes to remind me, too busy. We can't save the world, Lex. All we can do is make our corner a little bit better." She stood and put a lid on the snacks. "In fact, I'm late for a consult. Why don't you go down to the morgue and look at the body? It might give you closure. Or answers. I don't think the funeral home has made it by yet." With that, she disappeared down the hall.

An icy dread grew in the pit of my stomach. Going to look at a body just because seemed morbid and dark. And a hobby I didn't want to take up. I didn't know if I had clearance to do that. But I had questions. If I did a quick exam, I could put to rest the gossip and my own questions.

I took a deep breath and shimmied my shoulders, the movement carrying down to my hands. No time like the present. The morgue was in the hospital's basement, one floor below the Emergency Room and accessed by the service elevator.

The elevator doors opened. Shadows were heavy and the walls empty. No cute posters or community health initiatives advertised down here. I'd been here once, years ago, with a new employee tour. I followed my nose. No amount of chemicals could keep the scent of death from seeping out of the walls. To my right, a door was labeled "Morgue."

The small, windowless room featured a few dusty plastic plants. Their greenery a stark contrast to the dreary institutional beige walls. A woman sat at a scarred desk. She reminded me of a tiger's eye necklace my mom wore, worn and golden brown. On the desk sat a computer screen, stacks of paper, and a bobble head of a Smurf. I resisted the urge to bop it.

She looked up from a worn paperback novel. "What?" She touched the head and its head bobbed away. "Tell me a better example of greedy capitalism attacking peaceful citizens in search of more money. I'll wait."

I stuttered a wordless response. When I was a kid, I watched the cartoon every Saturday with a bowl of cereal in my lap. Coming down here might have been a mistake. Anyone who harbored thoughts so deeply about a cartoon was a person I might not identify—or be able to communicate—with.

She asked again. "What can I help you with?"

I smiled too wide and forced it down. I was trying too hard. "Hi, I was on the code team for Buffy Stephens. Would it be possible for me to… pay my respects to her?" My hand fidgeted with a loose string on the side of my pants.

The woman's brow furrowed for a moment. "I understand. Probably awkward if you show up at the funeral and explain to the family who you are." She stood. "We don't get many visitors down here but, in this case, I think it's fine." She waved me towards a metal door with a window at the top. "It's usually just me and the technician. He's at the gym right now."

After she scanned her badge, I followed her through the door into a stainless-steel room. One stainless steel table sat in the middle of the tiled floor. Another desk, this one metal, stood off to the side. Steel doors lined one wall and the other with jars of chemicals. She opened a metal door and pulled the tray out. The black plastic of the body bag held an impossibly slight frame.

The woman's shoulder dropped on the exhale. "I'll give you a few minutes." She strolled out of the room. The door closed with a soft click.

My arms hung at my sides as I stared at the tray. I exhaled hard and lifted my shaking hands to unzip the bag and push it aside. Buffy Stephens. Fourteen years old. So small for her age. Her blonde hair had been brushed and tucked behind her head. Her skin had lost its blush of youth. Now it was pale gray with veins visible. I choked back tears. She had an entire life ahead of her and something, or someone, had taken it from her.

A clean laceration on her neck cut her flesh from ear to ear. It was too clean. Almost surgical. No way an animal had done that. Bruises from the collar bone to her jaw continued down her arms and upper legs. I held my breath as I bent closer. They were so close together it was impossible to determine what caused them. On her arms, the bites appeared shallow. More tentative, than deliberate. I held up my hand against them to compare size. The bites appeared smaller than the palm of my hand. Wider than longer.

Her mid-section featured more bruising and another large incision. Not a bite or a tear, but an intentional cut, like with a knife or another sharp instrument. My brows knitted. The leg wounds were as I remembered them, torn and ragged, one injury blending into another.

Tears forgotten, I replaced the sheet over her and pushed the tray back into the cabinet with fresh resolve. The cafeteria forgotten. I wouldn't be eating for a while. The aging Dr. Nakamura hadn't done his job.

This was no animal attack. This was human.

Chapter Four

My hands fiddled with my scrub top and my badge pin as I paced in front of the elevator. Why were the police and the coroner so quick to close the case? "This isn't right," I whispered to myself.

In the elevator, I pulled out my cell phone and texted Scott.

—Hey, I viewed Buffy Stephen's body. Exactly what about it makes you think it's an animal attack?—

The elevator dinged for my floor, and I walked back to the nurse's station. I checked my phone periodically throughout the rest of the shift, but no response came from Scott. He finally responded when I dropped myself into my car.

—That's what the coroner's report said. Eyewitness agreed. Case closed.—

My neck stiffened as pain shot down my back while as I sat in the parking garage. I shook my head at his callousness. My fingers shook as I texted back.

—She has bruising and an incision on her neck from a knife, like a hunting knife or something big. Not to mention the condition of her abdomen. Did you review that? None of those are bites.—

His response was quick, leading me to believe he didn't give it much thought.

—Look, the case is closed. You don't like it, go to the Chief or the coroner—.

"Oh, really? That's your response?" My anger exploded in full burn. "Touché."

I typed a response, erased it, typed another, and erased that. Dropping the phone on the passenger seat, I huffed. "If I don't like it," I huffed again. "Guess if I want it done right, I have to do it myself."

I drove home and quickly changed into a long tunic and dark jeans and smoothed out my ponytail. The drive to the police station gave me time to debate whether I should have made an appointment with the Chief of Police. He was a family friend and once coached my high school soccer team. I might get away without an appointment.

The Atherton Police Department was housed in a small brick building off the town square that had once held all the city offices. Most of the departments had recently moved to a modern building next door but the police stayed. I parked out front and marched inside.

I went to high school with the guy at the desk, but I couldn't remember his name. I gave him the friendliest smile I could find after a ten-hour shift and was ushered right into the Chief's office.

"Lexi! How long has it been?" Chief Timothy Wagner walked around his desk with his arms out for a hug.

I embraced his scarecrow frame and expected a rustle of dried corn stalks. My memories of him weren't of this dry and brittle man. The scent of his bay aftershave enveloped me. I took the seat across from his desk. "Too long. How's Sarah?" His daughter Sarah had played soccer with me.

"She's good, she's good. Living up in Minnesota with her husband and kids." He dropped into the chair and leaned back with a groan. "Don't get to see her or the little ones enough." He shrugged. "How are your parents doing? They retired down to Florida, right?"

I nodded. "They're doing good. Getting tans. Thanks for asking." My parents had looked forward to retirement my entire life. Truth was, they hated every minute.

The Chief's gaze narrowed. "Did you come by just to catch up?"

I smiled. "Not wholly. Although it's good to hear Sarah's doing well. I stopped by to talk about Buffy Stephen's murder."

His face scrunched up. "Murder? I don't think we're calling it a murder. Animal attack is what Nakamura, and the detective, came up with."

"Right, that's what I've heard. But has anyone examined the remains? There's evidence it wasn't a simple animal attack. The incisions aren't bites. There are bruises on her—"

"Excuse me." He cut me off and held up his hands. "You looked at the body?" Immediately, I was transported back to my youth. His tone was on its way to full blown anger.

"I did. I was on the code team that tried to save her," I disclosed carefully. "I have concerns about the way they have handled things. The investigators and the coroner, I mean."

He leaned forward and rested his forearms on the desk. "I respect what you do, Lex, I really do. It can't be easy to see death and suffering day in and day out. Hell, Stephens was the first death we've had in... what... almost twenty years." He frowned. "But that still doesn't give you the right to desecrate a corpse."

My throat tightened and my shoulders scrunched up to my ears. A muscle or nerve misfired in my back that sent a spike pain of through me. "No one desecrated a corpse. I had questions and— – "

He interrupted me again. "You had questions and decided the official answers weren't good enough. You were going to get the genuine answers. Is that it?" His volume rose. "Your opinion is better than Dr. Nakamura's and your boyfriend's?" Contempt oozed with every syllable.

I held up my hands. "Look, Chief, I didn't mean to step on anyone's toes. I want what's best for Buffy and her family."

"But you did, didn't you? Step on people's toes. You always thought you were better than everyone else. Pretentious was the word used back then. You wouldn't take coaching then either." His chest puffed out. "Look. The case is closed. I suggest you go back to the hospital and wiping asses—or whatever it is you do over there—and leave the investigating to the professionals."

My chin rose. "I'd be happy to go back to my job, Chief, if only your professionals had done theirs." I stood and left the room, resisting the urge to slam the door.

By the time I got to the car, my vision was blurred, and my breath hitched in my throat. I'd forgotten how hateful Wagner could be when he wanted. He didn't care about that girl or her parents or the truth. I sat in the parking lot until my breathing evened out and the tears no longer flowed.

I pointed my car towards my house and let the thumping drums of a hair mental band song thrum through me. All I ever wanted was to help people. That's all I had to show for my life, no kids, a failed marriage, and a boyfriend on the outs. And now I can add being verbally sucker punched by the Chief of Police. Four-letter words and curses on his soul filled my car.

The curses increased when I got to the front of my house and saw Scott's car blocking the garage. I forgot to get my key back from him. I parked next to his car and continued cursing and grumbling, grabbed my tote, and schlepped to the front door.

Inside, I dropped my tote and kicked my shoes off with force and slammed the door. Scott stood with his back to the living room, a kitchen towel thrown over his shoulder, head down while he worked. The man could make award winning chili, but last time he'd cooked anything else the chicken was raw, and the potatoes burnt. I still didn't see how he managed it. Take-out containers littered the kitchen island. I sighed with relief. My digestive system was safe for another day.

He understood the way to my heart was through my stomach. He might not say the words "I'm sorry" but the food made up for it. If there was chocolate cake anywhere in the containers, I might forget everything and agree to marry him right here.

"You just walk into strange women's houses now?" I challenged.

"Hey, you." His head was down and raised his gaze to mine. Scott dropped saucy ribs on the plate. "I thought I'd bring you dinner." He dished up potato salad next to the ribs.

I plopped down on a barstool at the island and grimaced. "You realize I don't like ribs." I would not make this easy for him.

His jaw worked. "I got some chicken, too." He grabbed another tin foil covered container and piled blackened chicken slathered with sauce on a plate. "I learned you had a rough visit to the station."

My head dropped back. "Ugh, not you, too."

He passed me a plate. "Look, I'm not trying to gang up on you. When I texted you I didn't expect you to barge into Wagner's office. I appreciate you two go way back, but what possessed you to walk in? The Chief said he was going to charge you with trespassing and desecration of a corpse."

My fist slammed on the island, hard enough to rattle the plates and send the decorative vase filled with faux flowers banging against the wall. "Could we not do this right now? I'm hungry and not in the mood to listen to you and Chief Wagner talk about all the crimes I've supposedly committed or the ones you choose not to investigate."

"Wait, a damn minute. I'm here to make peace. I brought you the best BBQ chicken in town. What have I missed here?"

I pushed my plate aside and rested my forearms on the island, no longer hungry. "Why do I bother texting you if you don't pay attention? Did you even look at Buffy Stephens' body before closing the investigation? If you had, you would have the same questions I have. Or I hope to heaven you would."

His face reddened and his jaw tightened. "I didn't need to. Nakamura's report said cause of death was an animal attack." He shrugged. "It's no different from if he says cause of death is a car accident. He's the expert. That's what the people of this county elected him to do. That's what he gets paid for."

I swallowed hard. "You take his word for it? What about the bruises on her neck and arms?" Scott's brows rose. "What about the clean incision on her neck? No animal did that. Unless Fido suddenly developed opposable thumbs."

"Hold on, there's a cut on her neck?" He shook his head. "I don't remember seeing that in the report. The only things mentioned were bites from an unknown source, likely an animal."

"Or apparently you missed what I mentioned in my text. I'm not surprised at his half-assed report; Nakamura is half blind. Why he keeps getting elected coroner is beyond me." I sat back in the chair. "Probably because no one runs against him."

Scott walked around the island and took me in his arms, dropping a kiss on top of my head. "I'll look into it right now. I didn't come here to pick a fight with you. And you're right. Nakamura is not always thorough. I should have at least looked at the body. That's on me." My body relaxed in his comfortable embrace as I savored his warmth. "And as for us…"

I interrupted him by patting his arm. "Let's give it some time, okay? Let things settle." I wasn't sure I wanted to completely end things with him. "Thank you for dinner."

His bright stare held mine for a moment before he released me and moved towards the door. "Wait, take the ribs," I yelled. We divided the food into the tin containers and exchanged a sweet kiss goodbye at the door.

In the kitchen, I grabbed my plate and curled up on the couch to watch reruns of a vampire show. It was hours later when I had thrown my bra across the back of the couch and was dozing when my phone dinged. Scott had been busy.

—You were right. Definitely more going on than an

animal attack. I'm reopening the case—

"Hell yes," I said to my phone and dropped it back on the coffee table. I drifted off to sleep with a smile on my face. I might be pretentious, but I got shit done.

Chapter Five

The admission of a psych patient soon replaced the gossip about Buffy Stephens. The poor slob had been running around the local community center nude and smeared with honey after taking a half a bottle of the popular ED remedy and screaming about having to impregnate the universe.

At the end of my shift, I checked my phone. Zelda took a half day from teaching and asked if today was the day for happy hour. My fingers couldn't move fast enough to respond yes. By the time I slid behind the wheel, we'd decided on Mulligan's for deep fried goat cheese. My mouth watered.

Zelda sat at a high table in the bar with a drink in front of her. I dropped my tote in the empty seat and pulled myself into the chair. The server arrived immediately, and I ordered a beer and the goat cheese appetizer. Zelda added a few more appetizers to the order as well.

"Thanks for texting. I keep meaning to get with you, but time gets away from me."

Zelda nodded, her black curls bobbing around her head and took a drink from her margarita. "I understand. In the morning I have so many plans, but by the end of the school day I'm done. Am I getting old or am I in the wrong career?"

I laughed. My feet ached from running around the

unit for ten hours. My back spasmed from moving uncooperative patients and bending over bedsides because the automatic lift function broke down last year and hadn't made it to the repair shop. We're always understaffed and overworked.

"I get it. We both might be in the wrong line of work." The server dropped off my beer and I took a deep swallow. "Or maybe we're just ready for a change."

"Don't get me wrong. I love teaching. The kids are great, but recently... it's not the same. Buffy's death hasn't helped." She frowned and took another drink. "If I'm going to be honest, it's been off for a while."

"How are you doing with her death? How are the students taking it?"

"They brought in grief counselors from Kansas City, but the kids don't know them, so why would they talk to a stranger?" The appetizers were delivered to the table, and we dug in. "Death is hard at any age, but an animal attack?" Her cheek bulged with chips and spinach dip. "How do you explain that to the students? Cancer? I can do that. A car accident? I got that. But this? I got nothing."

"Did you teach the other girl, the one who found Buffy?"

She nodded. "Neveah. She was in my remedial English for two years. She struggled, but if you turned on music, she could tell you everything about it. From Mozart to Taylor Swift. Girl would have been a killer radio DJ back in the day."

I took a slow sip of the beer. "Could she have anything to do with it? Besides finding Buffy?"

Zelda watched the bartender wipe down glasses and refill sodas at the bar. "No. Neveah had some rough times, but she's a good kid."

"Could someone have gotten her mixed up in something, though?" I questioned around a cauliflower floret dripping with hot, creamy goat cheese.

Zelda frowned. "No. She might struggle with a lot of stuff, but she has a good head on her shoulders. Just enough religion to keep her on the straight and narrow." Zelda wasn't a fan of organized religion, but the town was big on it. It wouldn't do well if the parents realized she was more pagan than Pentecostal.

I wiped my hands on a napkin and prepared to tell my thoughts on Buffy's death. Zelda had been my best friend since elementary school and understood me better than anyone. I chugged the reminder of the beer and signaled the server for another.

"If I tell you something, you have to promise not to say anything to anyone." I leaned across the table. If I had a dollar for every time Zelda or I had said that phrase, we'd both be millionaires. And of course, anyone didn't mean our moms.

Zelda popped a cheese ball in her mouth and leaned forward. "What's up?"

I cleared my throat and started. "An animal did not kill Buffy Stephens. It was a person." Zelda's eyes widened. "I saw the body."

She sat back, her gaze on the food. She was silent for a long time before clearing her throat. "So, the coroner, police. They're all wrong?"

I nodded. "Scott said he'd reopen the investigation, but…"

Zelda held up a hand to interrupt me. "Nope, Buffy was one of my students. If anyone is going to find out who killed her and avenge her death, it's me. I will not let the males of this town forget about a girl's death. Men are too quick to forget the females who have passed on. Hell, most of the time they don't pay attention to the ones here. Even if we are the ones that birth them, bath them, marry them, and bury them."

Zelda fired up was hard to put out. Her current boyfriend of several months, Nate Winchester, didn't strike me as more than dating material. "When was the last time you did any of those things to a man?"

"That's not the point. The point is it's up to us women to look after each other. Whether in this life or the next."

I had seen the steely look in Zelda's eyes before. It usually came on at the local franchise Italian place and once at an ill-chosen rock-climbing outing. There would be no talking her out of this. She leaned her elbows on the table and popped a boneless buffalo wing in her mouth. "So, where do we start?"

I shrugged, unsure of where to start to investigate a murder. "We give Scott time to look into it and go from there."

She drained her margarita. "Good call. And you can wile info out of him in bed. People will give anything up for oral."

I wiggled my eyebrows. "Is that what you do with Nate?"

Zelda sniffed. "If he had info I wanted, I would. As it is, he's too quick to give it up. Sometimes a girl likes to work for it."

"Eh, not sure that'll work with Scott right now. I may have told him he didn't value human life, among other comments about his character flaws, so things are kinda up in the air right now."

"Again?" She shrugged. "All the more reason for oral. He'll think it's an apology and you'll get info. Win win."

I shoved a quarter of pita bread with hummus in my mouth and chewed. "That might work. But he brought ribs over the other night."

Zelda grimaced. "Ugh, doesn't he know you don't like ribs?"

"Exactly, seriously though, it might be time to break up. I'm not sensing the spark. It's just comfort. And I can't see myself sitting next to him in a rocking chair on the porch together in our old age."

"Well then, dump his ass. Don't waste your time. We're too old to mess around." She waved a dismissive hand and the stack of bracelets on her wrist played a melody. "I say that and can't see myself growing old with Nate, either. He's not even that good in bed. But he makes a mean meatloaf and cleans the hell out of a toilet."

We both agreed being an excellent cook and cleaner was important but debated their merits against good lover qualities. With inside jokes older than our server, we laughed until we cried. Hours later, we waddled out of the restaurant.

I hugged Zelda in the parking lot and promised I'd keep her in the loop on Buffy's death investigation.

"Don't wait too long on Scott solving anything. I have a vibe we'll have to do this on our own." Zelda pulled a small bag that smelled of lavender and other herbs I couldn't easily identify out of her purse. "Keep this under your pillow every night. It'll absorb all those bad pictures in your head."

I raised an eyebrow. "How did you know?" Zelda's

beliefs were something I still hadn't gotten used to. But she always meant well.

"Your aura is off, babe. Don't forget, under the pillow." I watched her slide behind the wheel of her beat up sedan and returned her wave. As long as I had her on my side, I knew we'd get to the bottom of Buffy's death.

Chapter Six

I barely dropped my tote in the front door when my phone buzzed with a text from Scott.

—*You were right about Buffy Stephens. Can I come over?*—

I was too full of cheese and chicken wings to entertain tonight but remained curious.

—*Do you have suspects?*—

—*Possibly, it's still early.*—

I snorted. I recognized a deflection when I heard one. He either had nothing or he only thought of one thing. Sighing, I sat on the couch. I had been hard on him and more emotional than I should have been. Or did I persist in making excuses for holding him accountable? Here I relaxed in my own house, over forty, and still trying to figure out men. I cursed under my breath and texted him back.

—*Went to happy hour with Zel. Come over if you want.*—

I deleted a smiley face emoji twice. Self-awareness was a bitch.

****

An hour later, I snuggled on the couch in my pioneer night gown, freshly scrubbed, and muscles relaxed when the doorbell rang. I groaned and pushed the blanket off before Scott walked in wearing a hoodie and jeans. He held a six-pack of beer up for my inspection.

"Hey beautiful." He dropped a kiss on my lips and took the beer to the kitchen. The scent of his aftershave lingered. "Did you and Zelda have a good time?"

I followed him into the kitchen. "Yeah, she had Buffy and the girl who found her in class."

I grabbed a glass and filled it with water from the fridge door. The beer looked good, but I'd regret another drink at this hour. When I was younger, I could drink the stock of an entire liquor store and still be up for class the next morning. Those days had long passed. Now, I'd paid for the two beers at happy hour for at least a day.

Scott cracked opened a beer and took a guzzle. "It's not a surprise. Isn't she like one of the five teachers at the high school?"

I walked back into the living room and curled up with the blanket. "Just because Atherton is small doesn't mean there are no educators." I hated to admit it, but Zelda's coworkers numbered less than twenty.

Scott took a seat next to me on the couch and grabbed the remote, turning the television to a sports channel. My head almost spun off my neck. I didn't go to his house and turn the television to a streaming service. I bit my tongue and did a mental calculation. Any day now I should start my period. That would explain my frustration, emotions, and the urge to kill over a remote. I hate it when he was right.

I attempted to tone down my harshness. "So… do you have suspects or what?"

He reached for my feet under the blanket and gave them a squeeze. "There's a few people I'm looking at. Nothing hardcore." His thumb massaged the spot of my feet that is always sore and achy. "But I'm doing my due diligence."

I resisted the urge to moan as he applied more pressure and focused on the conversation. "Who are you looking at?"

"We checked into the girl who found Buffy. Nothing there. Looking into Stewart."

"Celeste?" I asked, interrupting him. Celeste Stewart was a frequent flier at the hospital for a couple of self-induced conditions and a few God given.

His fingers slid over my foot, hit the usual tight spots. "They found the girl on her property. She was home but didn't see or hear anything." He took another swig of beer.

"I know Celeste. She couldn't hurt a fly. Or honestly, give much of a coherent statement." From personal experience, she wasn't the best self-reporter. Some of the medical staff suggested a move to assisted living for her but most of us knew her stubbornness and independence is what kept her going. "What about the dog or animal? Did you find any evidence of it? Any tracks?"

He took another deep draw and let out a loud burp. I couldn't judge. The cheese already making a reappearance for me. "It had rained that afternoon and the whole yard was covered in layers of leaves. I am looking at a dude, Condor, something or another. He runs a haunted house on the west side of town by the old warehouses during October and was the last one to see Buffy alive. Talking to him tomorrow."

Whether it was the foot rub or his smooth smile, I accepted his answer. For now. He was doing stuff on the case. Even if it seemed like he was going through the motions, it was a start.

Scott's hand traveled up my leg, higher, under my

nightgown. A familiar warming spread through my body. Cheese forgotten, and I sunk under Scott as he moved on top of me. His lips found mine, and a moan escaped my lips.

"You're still interested, even in the pioneer nightgown?" I asked, chuckling.

"We can role l play." His voice honeyed warmth along my spine. "I'll be the intrepid explorer." His hands pushed up the fabric and his fingers found the spot that made me forget Buffy, the nightgown, Zelda's suggestions, and the cheese.

****

The next morning, I felt as old as Methuselah. I stumbled to the bathroom, thankful for the blackout curtains in my bedroom. Scott was already up and dressed in his clothes from last night. I resisted the urge to get back into bed and slipped a robe on. The pioneer nightgown laying somewhere between the living room and the bed.

"See you tonight?" he asked, dropping a kiss on my lips.

"I might have some stuff to do." I wrapped my arms around his waist. "Text me. I'm off the next four days."

He gave me a squeeze. "Really?" I nodded. "You won't know what to do when you go back."

"Haha."

People always thought nurse's schedules odd and a sweet deal, but we worked our asses off. Trust me, more days off equaled better nurses. You don't want a worn down or pissed off nurse in charge of your care.

"Have a good one," I said as we released each other, and I waved at him as he left.

In the kitchen, I grabbed an iced coffee from the

fridge and chugged it, hoping it would wake me up. The bed was still more inviting than anything else I had to do today. When my phone buzzed for a facetime call, I groaned out loud and cursed creatively. That meant only one thing, my parents.

I took a deep breath, ran a hand through my hair, picked up the phone, and clicked answer. "Hi Mom!" I faked chirpiness and plastered a smile on my face.

My mom's frizzy gray hair created a halo around her face that filled the screen. "Alexandra, honey? Is that you?" She adjusted her glasses as her gaze searched the screen.

I resisted the urge to roll my eyes, knowing soon enough I might be in her place. "Mom, is the screen on? Can you see me?" I waved my hand across the screen.

She squinted and looked down her nose. "Hmmm…you look tired. I didn't recognize you, honey. Are you sleeping?" She frowned and shook her head. "And you're so pale! Ugh, you need to come to Florida. Get some sun, see me and your father, maybe meet a nice man."

I couldn't contain the eyeroll this time. "Mom. I am sleeping, it's been a busy of couple weeks. And I'll take some time soon and come visit you and Dad. I promise. Really."

"Uh huh. What's going on with that man?" Her face twisted up in dislike. "What's his name? Mark?"

"Scott, Mom. He's fine. Everything is fine." My parents had met Scott before they moved to Florida. Several times. And yet she still insisted she couldn't remember his name. "What's going on in Florida?"

My mom huffed. "Well, your father joined a swim club at the rec center. Bunch of old men acting like that eighties movie. Running around like they have a fountain of youth. In speedos." She rolled her eyes. "The other day your father came home and told me he's been working on his diving. No concern for me. Whatever, they're having fun."

I grabbed another iced coffee. "And you? What are you up to?"

"Me? Nothing, really. I have been busy writing letters to Congress and such. You know they're doing some crazy things."

"Uh huh, what about a club? Didn't you want to join the garden club or something?" It was too early and not enough coffee to talk politics with my mom.

She frowned again. "I joined a Mah Jong group but kept losing money. Those old women are sharks. And they cheat."

My phone buzzed and a showed a text from Zelda.

"Ooops, Mom. Gotta go. Zelda and I have plans today."

A smile brightened her face. Growing up if I wasn't at Zelda's house, she was at mine. My mother adored her. "Oh, tell her hello. And that I miss her! She should come to Florida with you."

"Will do, Mom. Love you."

"Don't forget about our cruise, honey. We'll text you when we get back, okay? Love you!" She fumbled with the phone, the screen flipping to the ceiling. "Love you! Tell Zelda hello and we love her!"

"Okay, I will. Love you." I clicked end and opened Zelda's text.

—What are you doing today?—

I took another chug of coffee; the sugar and caffeine hit me. I closed my eyes and groaned. I never want to experience life without coffee and sugar. My phone dinged again.

—*Waiting for you. What adventure do you have planned today?*—

I debated about how to respond. She didn't need any trouble as a teacher. Parents always seemed on the hunt for something to get a teacher fired. But she was the smartest person I ever met, and I wanted her by my side.

—*I'll be at your house in half an hour. Breakfast and then shenanigans.* -

I got a thumbs up emoji on my text and a Giff of a little girl with a devilish smile.

In the closet, I grabbed a pair of leggings and a long tunic. I pulled my hair into a low bun and swiped on a deep burgundy lip gloss.

As soon as I pulled into Zelda's driveway, she bounced down the steps. She lived in an older neighborhood where most of the homes were on the historic registry. Her neat brick house featured white shutters and flower boxes at every window. Zelda's green thumb could make flowers grow in the Sahara. Mine tended to die before they made it home from the garden center.

She jumped in and the scent of her soap and perfume filled the car. "Hey girl."

"Hey," I said, pulling out of the driveway and headed towards our regular brunch spot. I already smelled the grease from the Monte Cristo I would order. "What's up?"

Zelda shook her head. "Not a thing. Got the laundry done and picked up the house." She shrugged. "I'm all yours until Monday morning at seven a.m."

We both laughed. When we were kids, we always

dreamed of being archeologists like Indiana Jones or hunting ghosts. We fantasized about leaving our everyday lives of schoolwork and heading off into an adventure most of our lives, long before reality shows made it look cool and exciting.

"By the way, my mom says hello and we should visit her in Florida soon." I informed her as we parked and walked to the restaurant.

"Nice, I've always loved your mom. I'll definitely go to Florida with you, especially if she makes me those eggs and fried hot dogs for breakfast."

"I'm sure she will." There were times growing up when I believed Zelda was only friends with me for my mom's cooking. Those days have passed. Mostly.

We got seated fast and ordered. I got another iced coffee and water in a nod to my kidneys. Zelda got a large Bloody Mary that I hoped would make her more accessible to my suggestion.

"I can't wait for Scott. So, for today… want to look into Buffy's murder?" I asked, playing with my water glass.

"Hell yes!" Zelda shouted enthusiastically before glancing over her shoulder to make sure no one heard her. She leaned across the table, her voice a conspiratorial whisper. "What do you have in mind? I thought we were going to let Scott do this thing.?"

My mouth screwed up and I twisted my napkin. "I know that's what I said but something's not sitting right. Don't get me wrong, he's doing stuff, but I don't think it'll hurt if we look into it on our own. Anyway, he mentioned a few suspects last night."

She nodded knowingly and her gaze twinkled. "The blow job worked."

My face reddened and a sarcastic laugh escaped me. "Stay focused horn dog. One suspect is Celeste Stewart."

The server delivered our food. The Monte Cristo for me and Eggs Benedict for Zelda. "I'm not a horn dog. I simply enjoy earthly pleasures." She winked. "We should go talk to her. Maybe take something," Zelda suggested between bites of poached egg.

"Yes, and Neveah, too. Where does she hang out?" I popped a French fry into my mouth.

"Pretty sure she still lives off Franklin Lane with her mom. Her little sister is in my creative writing workshop at zero hour, and she hasn't mentioned moving or any changes in the home."

"Scott mentioned a Connor, or Condor, or something. Does that ring a bell?"Zelda shook her head. "Doesn't sound familiar."

"All right, let's eat, grab some sweets or something, and head to their houses. We should hit Celeste's first. I think she still takes afternoon naps."

Zelda's forehead wrinkled. "Might that be why she heard nothing when Buffy was murdered?"

"Good question. We'll find out."

We finished our plates and caught up on each other's weekly drama. I leaned back impossibly full and glad we only brunched a couple times a month. More than that and I'd have to be rolled out.

Chapter Seven

"Ugh." I rubbed my swollen stomach. "Why do I always eat so much?"

Zelda and I stood on the sidewalk in front of Atherton's few small businesses, squinting against the sunlight. "Because it's so good?" She donned a pair of sunglasses. "What are you thinking we should take Celeste to get her to talk?"

My face scrunched up. The nurse's side of me said a fruit plate, but the realist in me said a pastry. "She's partial to sweets, specifically maple bars."

Zelda tossed her hair over her shoulder. In the sunlight, the streaks of gray were more pronounced. I shuddered to think of mine. "Perfect, I could use a carb or two."

As we headed in the bakery's direction when my phone buzzed with a message from Scott.

—*Investigation is done. Everyone is cleared and I've confirmed it was an animal attack.*—

I handed the phone to Zelda for her to read the text. "Read the latest load of BS from the Atherton PD."

Her eyebrows raised in surprise. "Wait, what? Just like that it's over. Seems like your intuition is on target."

"Well then, guess it's a good thing we already had a plan in place." We walked to the bakery and loaded up on baked goods.

Our first stop was to Celeste Stewart's house. We

parked at the curb and walked up the broken sidewalk to the front door. Large branches of overhanging trees shaded the side yard from the midday sun where Buffy had been found. Crime scene yellow tape fluttered against the house's sagging porch.

We rang the doorbell, but the house was silent. Zelda raised her fist, and the door shook from the knock. We exchanged a glance and waited.

"She's not home?" Zelda said, raising her hand again.

I shook my head. "Her medications and groceries are delivered. She only leaves to go to the clinic, and it's closed today. She might be in the ER or urgent care."

Just as Zelda prepared to knock again, the door opened a crack. A yellowed eyeball in the middle of a wrinkled face peered out at us. "What do you want?"

"Hi Celeste, it's Lexi Burns from the hospital." I asked in my friendliest voice. "How are you doing today?"

The door opened another inch more. Celeste stared hard at us. "You making house calls now?" Suspicion oozed with each word. Her stare slid to Zelda. "Who's that with you?"

I held up the box from the bakery and pointed the clear top that showed the decorated pastries inside. "This is my friend Zelda. She teaches at the high school. We just thought with all the stuff going on lately, you might use a treat and a bit of friendly conversation."

The door opened wide, and Celeste took the box from my hands, gazing in the window. "Maple bars." Her lips smacked together. I fought down my grimace. "All right, come on in," she replied over her shoulder and shuffled through the small entrance way to the living room.

We followed her inside and took seats on a loveseat against the wall. Celeste plopped down in the threadbare recliner and a large, long-haired cat jumped on her lap. I remembered an incident from a few months ago where she, claiming a deathly allergy to all pets, threw a fit because someone had a service dog in the hospital. Now, as the cat curled up on her lap, purring. I didn't feel so bad for bringing the maple bars.

Celeste opened the box, lifted one out, and took a big bite. Her eyes rolled back in her head, and she let out a loud moan. Zelda stifled a laugh.

I cleared my throat, pulling Celeste away from the sugar rapture. "How have you been, Celeste?"

She popped the last bit of pastry into her mouth and gave her fingers to the cat to lick. "Not too bad. Been too much excitement the past couple of days."

Zelda spoke. "It must have been terrible for you."

Worse for Buffy, but I kept my mouth shut.

Celeste nodded. "Yes, horrible. All the noise and commotion." She waved a hand in the air. "People tramping all over the place. And that poor girl. It took the police hours to tell me she had passed."

Zelda eyebrows scrunched together. "It must have been very upsetting." Celeste agreed, and Zelda continued. "Did you see anything that day? Hear anything?"

Celeste petted the cat on her lap, and it purred with contentment. "Not a thing. I was sitting here watching my afternoon shows. The TV was up loud, cause my hearing aid's been on the fritz. I might have been dozing off. The other girl's screaming woke me up. I about wet myself. Sounded like she was in the room with me."

"That loud?" I asked. The windows in this room were on the opposite side of the house from where the girl was found. That meant Celeste would have had to hear the screams through the window, the bedroom, the wall, all with the blaring television. She didn't wear her hearing aid often and if it was malfunctioning, I didn't see how she heard the scream. Even an individual with good hearing might have a hard time hearing.

Celeste's hand stroked the cat's dark fur. "I figured it was kids playing out there. Lots of them cut through my side yard to the gas station down the street. But the scream happened again. Got me out of the chair and out the back door. I couldn't get down the stairs too fast, but the girl ran to me."

"Neveah?" Zelda asked. "The red-haired girl?"

Celeste nodded. "Yep, she ran up and almost knocked me over. Before I figured out what she was saying, the police showed up."

Scott said a neighbor had called the police. I assumed it was Celeste but if one of the others had heard something they might have called it in first. But why hadn't he mention anyone else and their proximity to the crime scene?"

"I gave her a glass of water and waited until the police came in," Celeste said. "She wouldn't stop blubbering."

"About what?" Zelda inquired. "What did she say?"

"Something about a werewolf."

"What?" I moved to the edge of my seat, curious. Zelda's leg bounced against mine.

Celeste eyed another maple bar. "She kept blubbering on and on that she'd seen it running away from girl, from the body." She shook her head. "But that's not possible. Girl watched too many scary movies is all."

"Of course," I replied and resisted the urge to remind Celeste of her recent diagnoses of type two diabetes as she dug into the second maple bar. This was just as much my doing though. I should have gone with the fruit plate.

Celeste continued. "It wasn't even a full moon." She swiped her finger through the icing and sucked it. "And the middle of the afternoon. Whoever heard of a werewolf in the middle of the day? Would've made more sense if she said it was a vampire."

"Miss Celeste, did you hear anything earlier? Like a little before the scream?" Zelda implored. She wanted something solid and so far, all we had was unsound. "While you were getting a drink or a snack?"

Celeste's face scrunched in thought. "Well, now that you mention it. Queeny here acted crazy… oh… a bit before. I went to the bedroom and looked out the window but saw nothing. Figured it was just the kids."

I did the timeline in my head. "That would have been after the school got out." I turned to Zelda, and she agreed.

"Miss Celeste, did you know Buffy Stephens? Had you seen her before?" Zelda asked.

Celeste shook her head. "I didn't know her but seen her cut through the yard enough times. She'd come back from the gas station with a bag of candy in her hand and a soda. She waved once or twice, seemed like a good kid. Didn't throw trash in the yard. Shouldn't have ended the way she did." Celeste wiped a hand across her eyes and squeezed the cat close. "No one should end that way."

Zelda cleared her throat. "You're right. She was a

good kid."

I sensed tears were close to falling, and that was something I avoided. Tears did nothing but show weakness. "Thank you, Celeste. If you think of anything else, would you call me at the hospital?"

Celeste nodded. "I sure will." She moved to lower the legs of the recliner, but I told her to stay comfortable. "Sure will. Thanks again for the sweets. And I'll make sure to make my insulin soon." She gave us a wink as we let ourselves out. Zelda locked the door behind us.

We said nothing until we got back in the car. "A werewolf? What the hell?" Zelda emphasized. "Could she have heard wrong? Misunderstood?"

"She sucks at reporting her symptoms and health issues but doesn't have a history of imagining things. And from my experience, she only misunderstands things when it suits her."

"You trust her?" Zelda asked as I slid behind the wheel.

"Yeah, I do. What does she have to gain by lying? It's pretty clear no one would consider her a real suspect, no matter what Scott said. Her mobility alone limits her. Let's go talk to Neveah. See what she has to say." I pulled the car away from the curb. "There's no such thing as werewolves."

Zelda gave me directions to a larger house few streets over. Pulling up in front, Fleetwood Mac blared from an upstairs window. "She loves music," Zelda explained as she left the car.

Chipped paint covered most of the house, obscuring the original color. The front wooden steps creaked under our weight. I raised my hand to knock when the front door opened. A lean young woman with flaming red hair stood in front of us. "Ms. Allen!" She threw open the flimsy screen door and grabbed Zelda in a hug.

Zelda returned the hug before pushing the woman away gently. "Neveah, how have you been?" The girl moved in for another hug which Zelda accepted briefly before putting her arms down and placing her large purse in front of her feet.

"So good, Ms. Allen. I missed you. Sometimes I check out the books we read in your class from the library. But it's not the same as when we read them with you." Neveah stepped back and dropped her arms. "How are you doing?"

Zelda smiled and took the second box of pastries from my hands. She held them out to Neveah. "I brought your favorite. It's still cookies and cream, isn't it?"

The girl's face lit up. "You never forget anything, Ms. Allen." She took the box and motioned for us to follow her inside. She sat it on small table in the combination kitchen/living room. "I'll save these for my mom if that's okay."

We both nodded.

"My mom loves cake and is working a double today." Neveah took a seat on the worn couch while we sat on another loveseat. "Ms. Allen, I can't believe you're here."

Zelda smiled. "With everything that you've been through this week, I wanted to check on you. Make sure you're doing okay."

The smile faded from Neveah's face, and her head dropped.

"Are you okay, Neveah?" Zelda inquired, her voice low.

Neveah kept her gaze on her hands in her lap. Her

voice began to quiver. "It's just everyone's thinks I'm lying and I'm not. I know what I saw."

"What did you see, honey?" I asked.

Neveah sniffed hard and raised her head. "I saw a werewolf eat a girl."

Chapter Eight

Our jaws dropped.

"A werewolf?" I asked, making sure my voice stayed even.

"Everyone's been making fun of me, even my mom." Neveah's face twisted in pain. "You don't know what you seen, you're just stupid, no good for nothing." Her voice mimicked the people that hurt her. "But I'm not." She shook her head violently. "I know." Her balled fist banged against her leg.

Zelda reached out and patted her knee, then took Neveah's hand in hers. "I believe you." When the tears continued, she said, "I trust what you say."

I went to the tidy kitchen, grabbed a glass out of the dish drainer and filled it with cold water, I brought it to Neveah.

"Even if it seems impossible, I have no doubts," I told her. "Because it's what you saw and if Zel—Ms. – Allen believes you, then I do, too. Can you tell us exactly what you saw?"

Neveah nodded and took a deep drink. She sighed hard. "I was cutting through Miz Stewart's side yard. I do that a couple times a week to go to the gas station and get a soda. I don't share with anyone though, it's a treat just for me."

"Treating yourself is nice, Neveah." Zelda patted her knee again. "It's good to do that."

Encouraged, Neveah's back straightened. "I was cutting through and noticed the thing. At first, I thought it was just a big ol' pile of leaves and the sunlight messing with my eyes. But then I saw the monster." She held the glass between her knees and brought her hands up to demonstrate size. "Like taller than a dog and hairy. Big. And it held the girl against itself, on the ground. Kind of on top of it. The leaves and house and the shadows and all made it hard to see but it was a monster. Plain as us sitting here."

"Were you in the front yard when you noticed the animal or were you by the house?" I remembered the shadows the trees threw around the house. If Neveah had been in the front yard, I don't know how she would have seen much of anything.

Neveah considered for a moment. "I was right at the house. I hadn't seen anything before. I said something or screamed, I don't know, and the werewolf turned and looked at me. I promise you. It was a werewolf. The eyes were human."

Zelda released Neveah's hands and dropped against the cushions. "Human eyes?"

Neveah nodded. "Yeah, like dog eyes are always sweet, you know? Like even a bad dog has dog eyes. But those eyes were mean. Dogs don't have mean eyes. That's how I know it was human."

Zelda's shoulder touched mine. "What happened when the thing turned towards you?"

"It dropped the girl and ran off towards the gas station. It ran on two legs, like a man. I didn't believe what I saw. Almost tripped on the girl, running after the monster. That's when I saw all the blood." Her voice hitched. "Miss Stewart was out on the back porch, and I ran to her. She took me inside."

"I'm so sorry you had to go through that, the ordeal must have been scary," I said. Clearly, Neveah was stronger than people gave her credit for.

She shrugged. "I don't know. I guess if the werewolf had come for me, I would have been scared. I was more scared when my mom's ex-boyfriend grabbed my butt." Neveah didn't have an easy life. She also didn't have a reason to lie.

"Thank you for explaining. I can imagine that this must be hard to talk about," Zelda acknowledged.

Neveah shrugged. "I'm okay. I try not to think about the monster, but…" She trailed off.

"What?" I asked.

Neveah fidgeted with a green beaded bracelet on her wrist, twisting the string back and forth. "Last night I swear I heard something outside my window."

"Like what?" Zelda scooted to the edge of her seat. If Neveah said barking, I was going to curse and google silver bullets.

She twisted the bracelet faster and shook her head. "Like a scratching and rustling. Like something was at the window. A growl? But my sister didn't make out anything, and my mom was still at work." She started rocking back and forth. "Might be I imagined the noise, but it seemed real."

"Would you call us if you hear anything again? We'll come by and check the commotion out."

Tears filled Neveah's eyes. "You would do that?"

Zelda and I both nodded. "Absolutely. We've got your back."

"Wow…I've never had anyone have my back before." She dropped the bracelet. "Do we do a blood oath or something?"

Zelda's head tilted to the side. "Not this time. Hand me your phone and I'll put our numbers in so you can call us whenever."

Neveah handed over her phone and Zelda added our contact information. We promised Neveah that we'd come whenever she needed us. I feared we'd be getting a text in the middle of the night tonight to check if we'd come over.

Zelda rummaged in her purse and pulled out a clear crystal wrapped in silver thread. It was about finger length and came to a wicked point at the end. She handed it to Neveah. "Take this, too. Keep it with you all the time." She closed Neveah's hand around the stone. "Even when you sleep, keep it next to you, got it?"

Neveah's eyes widened. She held the stone up and watched light prisms shift through the room. "Yes, Ms. Allen."

We said goodbye to Neveah just as her sister came home from the library. Zelda talked to her for a minute before we excused ourselves and headed to the car.

"You gave her your lucky crystal?" I quizzed Zelda as soon as we were out of earshot.

"Eh?" Her shoulders rose and dropped. "She needs it more than me. I'd bet she's having nightmares. And with the right force behind it, it'll do some damage if someone comes after her."

I agreed. My head swam from the conversations of the day. Nothing jumped out as a clue, but there was something there. I needed to consider the whole picture. Alcohol would help. "Want to grab a drink?"

Zelda shook her head. "I've eaten out once today. Can't again on what I make." She shrugged. "How about we grab some wine coolers and head back to your house?"

"Sure, or we could go to your house?"

"Nope. Nate keeps showing up as soon as I get home. I swear he has a tracker on me."

"Are you dating the guy or what?" I asked and headed for the liquor store. Nate Winchester was a teacher at Zelda's school and had been sniffing around her for years. After she broke up with her longtime boyfriend a couple months ago Nate swooped in.

"I think so?" Her statement was more a question. "He's always around. At school, home, everywhere. And he's not a bad guy but...I can't seem to get away." She shivered. "Ugh."

"Is it the way he dresses?" Nate was infamous for wearing collared silk shirts tucked into faded black jeans all the time. Although recently, the buttons had begun to gap dangerously. I couldn't remember when he was in fashion and had no idea where he bought his clothes.

Zelda sighed again. "I mean, that is an issue. I hoped he would change. Like that dude you dated that wore the socks with sandals? He changed." She held up her hands in defense. "I know I shouldn't try to change a man but it's just a shirt for hell's sake. It's like he's always there, suffocating."

I didn't have a problem with wanting to change someone's fashion. She didn't want to change his personality or how he acted. Socks and silk shirts don't make the man, after all.

Zelda agreed. In the liquor store we picked up a package of wine coolers and a bag of kettle chips before heading back to my house.

We popped open a few bottles and kicked up our

feet on the couch not really talking about anything until we'd had a few drinks.

"Thoughts on today." I took another sip of my berry cooler and curled under a blanket on one end of the couch.

Zelda stared straight ahead and was quiet. She was mulling things over. Unless you got her worked up, she took her time to respond, and each word mattered. After several weighty seconds, she said, "Celeste knows more than she's said." Zelda took a swig of her citrus cooler. "She doesn't move easy. How did she get from her recliner to the back porch so fast?" She shook her head. "No, she was already up and seeing what the ruckus was. She observed something."

"That makes sense. The timeline between her and Neveah doesn't mash up."

We sat in silence for a while.

"So curious about the animal," I said.

"You mean the werewolf?" Zelda popped a chip in her mouth.

"Was she prone to making stuff up when she was in your class?"

Zelda shook her head. "Nope, she struggled with any creative writing assignment. Even a sentence." She held up a finger next to her head. "The wheels turned. She struggled getting words out on paper. But give her a report to do and she'd ace it. She wrote for the school newspaper for a semester or two. Always spot on." Zelda burped quietly. "Pardon."

"So, a girl that has hardly any imagination and kills on facts said she saw a werewolf." I put a handful of chips in my mouth. "What does that equal?"

Zelda took a handful of chips and shoved them in her mouth. "The girl saw a werewolf."

Chapter Nine

"Careful, I almost spit out my drink." I chuckled and wiped my mouth with the back of my hand. "You seriously think she saw that?"

Zelda shoved another handful of chips in her mouth. "Absolutely. I'm not saying we go hunting for a werewolf, but we need to keep an open mind. There are other things out in the world, Lexi, that science can't or won't explain." Her phone dinged from its place on the end table near her. She ignored it.

"Not sure I agree." I popped another chip. "Science is the grounding force in the universe. I can guarantee the police didn't believe her."

"Nope, that's the law for you, girl. And they've officially closed the case?"

I grimaced at her loaded statement. Zelda was first in the protest line and first to fight for equal rights. I agreed with her but couldn't bring myself to get involved like she did. But I was always there to bail her out. I changed the topic. "Yeah, and I think I might be done with Scott."

Zelda's eyes got big. "You too? We'll be single gals together again." Her phone dinged again, and she read the screen and frowned.

The last time we were single at the same time was in our mid-thirties. I still cringe at the few memories from a weekend in Vegas. And the weekend at the lake.

And the weekend on the Florida Gulf Coast. I wasn't so sure my liver or my back could take weekends like those now.

"Ugh, Nate wants to stop by." She typed furiously. "I'll tell him no because I'm at your place." She sat the phone back down. "I don't know that I want to grow old with a man. Listening to them snore and fart the rest of my life." Zelda shivered. "I'd rather live in a house with you and maybe a couple of cats. Or dogs. But definitely no birds."

"Agreed." Thirty years later and we were still traumatized by a Hitchcock movie we watched at a slumber party. I glanced at my watch. It was almost nine. Not late, but time to take the bra off. I was on my second wine cooler and feeling it. "How about you spend the night? Get a jump on that old age thing?"

Zelda smiled and dropped her head back. "I thought you'd never ask. Between being sleepy and these," she held up the empty wine cooler, "I'm in no shape to get off this couch."

I stood and took our empties to the kitchen. "I'll get you a nightgown and your room should be ready. I'm going to change, and I'll be back."

A knock sounded at the front door. Zelda and I shared a concerned glance. "Are you expecting Scott?" With my feet rooted to the spot, I shook my head. The knock sounded again.

"Even if it was, Scott, he has a key," I whispered.

Zelda's eyes were wide, and her forehead scrunched. She stood. "Then who the hell knocks on a lady's door after dark?"

My hands played with the hem of my tunic, twisting the seam. This was ridiculous. We were grown women.

A rap at the door shouldn't scare us. I stomped to the door and threw it open, ready to tackle whatever was out there.

"Hey, sexy lady," said the man wearing the purple silk shirt in front of me. His long greasy hair was pulled back into a low ponytail, giving him either a founding father or a decades old disco vibe. "Zel's here, right?"

I had no words as he pushed past me, the heavy cloud of his cologne choking me.

"Nate? What the hell?" Zelda's face reddened. "What are you doing here?"

He dropped a kiss on her lips. "Babe. Your text said you were here, so I came by." He moved to wrap his arms around her. She leaned and sidestepped away.

"That doesn't mean you just stop by," she hissed through clenched teeth.

Unbothered, Nate reached for her again. "Babe, I wanted to see you."

"We'll talk outside." Zelda grabbed Nate's arm and dragged him out the door, closing it behind her.

I shook my head. "The audacity," I said to the empty room. The sound of low voices was barely audible through the door. I put my ear against it and strained to listen.

"This isn't Nate time. This is Lex time. Got it?" Zelda's tone was one I remembered from when she stood up to a bully in high school. I let out a low whistle.

"Why does Lex get priority over your boyfriend?" Nate's whine wouldn't win him any points with Zelda.

I dropped on the couch and wrapped up in the blanket and waited. It wouldn't be long. A few minutes later, the door opened, and Zelda walked in. Her face was twisted and flushed red. "You okay? You look like you ran a mile."

Her gaze threw flames as she joined me on the sofa. "See what I mean? It's like he always knows where I'm at."

I rolled my eyes. "You did text him."

"But not to come over!" She blew a raspberry and huffed. "Who does that? Just comes to someone's house? And he questioned me. No one does that. No one."

I agreed with Zelda but was tired. Best not to get her more riled up. "It's not like we're strangers. He's been here for game night and cook outs." I shrugged. "I'm going upstairs." I patted her leg. "Calm yourself down. I'll be back."

I came down fifteen minutes later to find Zelda on the couch snoring loudly. The remote was in her hand and the television was on a rerun of a medical drama. I slid the remote out of her hand and changed it to something more realistic, like a home repair show. If we were going to be single, retired ladies, we better be prepared. At some point, I dozed off and woke up to my cell phone buzzing. Fumbling for it, I struggled to focus my eyes on the screen. The text message from Scott made me moan, and not in a sexy way.

—*Want me to come over tonight?*—
—*No thanks, Zel's spending the night.*—.
—*Too much shopping today? Lol*—.
—*Something like that. TTYL*—

I added a heart emoji at the end and sent the text. As I listened to Zelda snore, I wasn't sure I wanted to live a life of celibacy just yet.

I set down the phone and started channel surfing. It was barely ten o'clock, and I refused to go to bed before ten, no matter how long I might snooze on the couch.

I speed clicked past a loud commercial and Zelda snorted herself awake. "What's?" she asked, still mostly asleep.

"Nothing exciting, just something called a spurtal."

She worked her mouth and frowned. "Ugh, I need water." She went to the kitchen and brought a glass of water back. "I hate to do this, but I'm going to bed. I don't care how early it is." She chugged the water.

I wrapped my robe tighter round myself. "Go ahead. I'll be up in a little while. I left a nightgown out on the bed for you."

Zelda patted my shoulder as she stumbled through the living room and up the stairs.

I channel surfed, found nothing of interest, and turned off the television and the lights before I headed to bed. I was taking my robe off when a scratching noise came from outside.

My heart stopped and froze. It was the shrubs against the side of the house. Chuckling to myself, I'd been meaning to have them trimmed for months. The sound came again. This time louder and closer to the window. There were no bushes directly under the window. I took a deep breath and moved closer, pulling the curtain back. My heart froze in my chest. There were no lights on this side of the house. My eyes strained to make sense of the shadows.

A large shape moved out from the bushes next to the house and towards the back. My feet moved. "Zel!" I yelled in the hallway and barged into her room. She turned over and groaned in my direction.

"What's wrong?" she slurred.

"There's something outside." My voice sounded small and scared.

She sat up in bed, breathing heavy. Even in the dark I could see her eyes were wide in the dark. The sound started up outside her window. The scraping was loud. Another sound joined it. Then a low growl.

There was something out there.

Chapter Ten

Zelda threw off the blanket and pushed me aside. She slammed open the window. "Hey, what the hell is going on out there?"

The growl sounded again, louder, animalistic. My muscles twitched. The neighbor's back yard lights turned on and spilled into my backyard. There, in the shadows, stood a tall, wide figure covered in fur. It uttered another grunt and threw its head back and howled.

"I'm too old for this shit. I need my sleep. Get out of here!" Zelda yelled. She turned to me. "Give me something to throw at this son of a bitch. It's just someone playing games."

I handed her the old analog alarm clock on the nightstand. She reared back and launched the clock at the creature. It made contact square on the head; it let out a decidedly human yelp. The figure took off running between the houses. "That's right, you better run!" Zelda shouted.

She turned and ran down the stairs, cursing the whole way. I stayed at the window, following the figure through the neighborhood, my eyes strained until it was swallowed by the darkness.

Zelda appeared in the backyard. "Where did he go?" she shouted up to me.

"Zel, no," But she was already across the yard.

My heart lurched in my throat. Images of Buffy's blood on my gloved hands froze in my mind. Zelda might have been strong when she was younger, but she threw her back out a couple of weeks ago sneezing. The clock throw was sheer luck. That thing would eat her alive or break her in two. I ran after her.

Houses down the street began to light up. Zelda ran on ahead. The light-colored nightgown flowed behind her, giving her a ghostly appearance.

I followed down a small alley between houses. Shadows enveloped me. My chest burned and my side ached. "Zelda," I whispered and gasped for air. There was no sign of her.

Scrub cedar bushes lining the alley swayed. My chest constricted. No wind blew. "Zel?" The word croaked out. "Zelda?"

A thick, musky scent hit me, and my stomach wrenched. I wheezed, trying to suck air in but the animal scent assaulted my throat and nostrils. A warm breeze like a fetid breath washed over me. The odor intensified. Alarms boomed in my head. Did Buffy smell this before she died? The bush shook again.

Red and blue strobe of police lights rounded the corner. Zelda cursed and gasped as she came back down the alley. The lights highlighted a large kitchen knife in Zelda's hand. The police car screeched to a halt just feet from us.

"Get your hands up!" the officer yelled before the car door opened.

The knife clattered to the ground and our hands flew up. The officer approached with gun drawn. "Lexi? Lexi Burns? Is that you?"

Relief flooded through me, and I barely nodded.

Officer Sarah Scully and I often crossed paths at a police bowling night with Scott. We'd talked about her time on the mean big city streets before she came to Atherton.

Scully holstered her gun. "What the hell are you doing out here?"

I spared a glance at the bush and gasped for a breath. It no longer moved. I croaked out something that might have been a word.

Zelda stepped in, sucking air in between each word. "A... creature in her yard. I threw a clock at it. It ran...I went after it."

"And that's why you have a huge ass knife with you?" Scully shined a light on the weapon.

Zelda shuffled her weight from foot to foot. "I wanted to see what the thing was, it could be what killed Buffy Stephans."

Scully shined the light up and down Zelda's light pink nightgown with bunnies on it.

"Uh huh. So, you took off after a creature, in a nightgown with a knife but not before you threw a clock at it. I want to make sure I get this straight."

Zelda rested her hands on her hips, chin in the air defiant. "Exactly. I got the knife to protect myself."

"Hands back in the air. I'm not a hundred percent sold on your story." Scully approached Zelda and picked up the knife. "Lexi, is that what happened?"

I nodded and cleared my throat. "Pretty much. Zel–Zelda spent the night. I heard something and woke her up and we ended up here."

Scully shook her head. "First the mauling and now you two running through a quiet neighborhood, scaring the hell out of everyone." She motioned for us to drop our arms. "Ya'll could have gotten yourselves killed.

71

You know how many people have gun permits in this neighborhood?" She shook her head again as the radio on her shoulder squawked. "Ya'll get in the car; I'll give you a ride home."

We got in the back of the patrol car, thankful for the warmth. The heat made my bare feet feel numb. Scully picked up the mic, "Scully here, car 6-18, I've got Lexi Burns and…" She clicked off the mic, looking over her shoulder at us.

"Zelda Allen," Zelda answered, too chipper for the situation.

Scully rolled her eyes and continued. "… and a Zelda Allen. Apparently, there was an intruder, and they took off in chase with a butcher knife. I'll return them to Burns' house." She clicked off the mic.

She pulled away from the curb when the mic lit up with an incoming message. A familiar voice asked, *"Lexi Burns?"*

I squeezed my eyes and groaned. Of course. Scott had the radio on. He left it on for background noise even when he slept.

Scully smirked at me and spoke into the mic, "The one and only."

His voice rasped across the line. *"Tell her I'll be at her house ASAP."*

Scully's gaze met mine in the rear-view mirror. "Copy that. 6-18 out."

A couple of streets later, we were back at my house. Scully turned to us. "I'll walk you inside." She let us out of the back and the three of us walked across the lawn. "Wait, the front door is locked." In my adrenaline drenched mind, I couldn't figure out how to get in the house.

Zelda headed around the side and waved us to follow. "We'll go in the way we left."

Scully and I followed her through the shadows. At the back of the house the door stood open to the kitchen, dark. Zelda came to a stop.

"You all just left the door open like that?" Scully asked, her hand on her weapon.

I glanced at Zelda. "This must be one of the stupidest things we've done. Why did we run out of the house in the middle of the night?" I gestured to the gaping darkness. "And leave the door open? For all we know that thing circled back and is lying in wait for us."

Scully headed to the back door. She freed her weapon. "I'll go through the house."

Zelda crossed her arms in front of her chest and returned my glance, unashamed. "Do you think she's going to give your knife back?"

I rolled my eyes. "That's what you're concerned about? You might have gotten killed tonight."

Zelda shook her head. "It's a good knife. I never got close enough to that thing, whatever it was. It ran like its ass was on fire." She stretched her back and rubbed her hips. "I'm gonna be sore in the morning."

"For your sake, I'm glad you didn't catch up. You need to be more careful." My teeth chattered. "How are we supposed to retire together if you die early?"

"I know I shouldn't have taken off. Hell, I shouldn't have yelled at the thing. I just got so mad. I need my sleep. Then I realized it probably is what killed Buffy, and I lost my mind." Her voice held a frustrated apology.

I wrapped an arm around her, and she rested her head on my shoulder. "Just be careful. You're not invincible."

Scully came back outside and holstered her weapon. "House is empty. You're good to go. Seriously though, I almost shot you both, you know that? Promise me neither of you will go running around like that again."

We both nodded. Scully said goodnight, and I agreed to look her up sometime to have a drink or coffee. We trudged inside and locked the door firmly behind us.

Zelda pulled a bottle of whiskey out of the fridge. She didn't bother with a glass, instead unscrewed the cap and chugged straight from the bottle. She winced and wiped her mouth with the back of her hand then handed the bottle to me. I held up my hand to say no. "That thing killed Buffy," she said, her voice stark. "I know it."

I dropped on the kitchen stool and laid my head on my arms. The kitchen was quiet except for our breathing and the sounds of sloshing whiskey.

My breath finally came back to normal. I raised my head and stared at Zelda. "I have no idea what that thing was, but it killed Buffy."

Zelda sat the bottle back in the fridge and turned to me. "Agreed. It doesn't make sense for there to be two strange creatures running around the same small town."

"Exactly," I said. "The real question is: what was it doing here tonight?"

Chapter Eleven

When the front door shook from a heavy knock, Zelda's hand moved to the butcher block knife rack.

"Oh, for heaven's sake, stop it." I walked to the door and checked the peephole. Scott stood there in sweatpants and a hoodie. I opened the door to him and said, "Hello, dear," putting as much pleasant into my voice as I could manage–and failed miserably.

He barged past me into the house. "What in the hell were you thinking?"

I closed the door, dropped my head against it, and sighed. Another issue Scott and I had. When he was angry, his preferred method of communication was mansplaining. He stood with his hands on his hips, head jutted forward. "The 911 reports said a homicidal maniac was running through the neighborhood with a butcher knife."

"That was me," Zelda said from the kitchen, leaning on the island. "I chased after the creature that killed Buffy Stephens." Like it was something you do every day. "Trying to catch the killer. Maybe you've heard of it?"

Scott stared at her a long time before making a sound of disgust. "I should have known you were involved."

I've been friends with Zelda for over thirty years and dating Scott for two. There was no love lost between the two. If push came to shove, it would always be her over him. You just didn't throw away a friendship like that over a dude. No matter how sexy or awesome in bed.

Zelda shrugged and turned her back on him, opening the fridge and inspected its contents.

"Look, there's no creature," he snarled between clenched teeth. "It was an animal. It will not happen again." When I opened my mouth, he raised a hand to stop me. "It was unfortunate. But it was an accident. She was at the wrong place at the wrong time. It's done, closed."

I crossed my arms in front of myself, colder from just from our experience outside. "I don't accept that."

He let out a dry laugh and looked at the ground, hands back on hips. "That's fine, sweetheart. Don't. But the next time you pull something like this, and you will with that one around." He pointed Zelda's direction. "I won't be able to do anything to help you. The Chief is already royally pissed about you desecrating a corpse, then for interrogating him, and *then* by going off to question witnesses. Are you nuts?"

"Wait, what about corpses?" Zelda peeked out from the fridge with a leftover container in one hand, a piece of chicken in the other.

I ignored her. "How did you learn about that?"

"It's a small-town, sweetheart. I know what you're doing twenty-three out of twenty-four hours a day."

"Really? If you spent more time investigating crimes and less in my business, I wouldn't have to do your job for you." Every word came out angrier than the last. The idea of someone knowing what I did all the time created an uneasy feeling deep inside my gut.

"Stop, just stop." His sigh carried a combination of

frustration and dismissal. "Everyone has signed off on the case. The funeral is scheduled. Stop acting like a junior detective. I can't smooth things over again."

Blood rose in my cheeks, and I pushed away from the door, closing the space between us. "I'm not some kid you need to monitor. I'm not a project." My voice was the dead quiet that normally made a medical resident pee themselves. It had little effect on Scott.

"Then act like it." There was no love left in his tone.

I returned to the door and opened it. "You are leaving."

We stared each other down, silence saying everything we wouldn't before Scott huffed and stalked out the door. I slammed the door so hard the panes in the adjacent window rattled.

Zelda appeared from the kitchen with two glasses of water and an eyebrow raised.

"Did he just do what I think he did?" She took a deep drink of water and passed a glass to me.

I chugged the glass. Refreshed, my anger didn't dissipate. With every blink, I was more offended. I dropped on the couch with a curse. "He absolutely did." I grabbed a blanket and wrapped up in it.

Zelda sat down next to me and pulled part of the blanket to cover her legs. "So that's done," Zelda said with finality.

"No."

She glanced at me with surprise all over her face. "We're not going to stop?"

I shook my head. "Not a chance in hell. We're going to keep going and find out what really happened to Buffy. Whatever that thing was tonight proves something happened more than what the officials say.

We're not giving up."

"Excellent. I don't want to give up. Buffy was a good kid." Zelda shook her head. "Not that it matters. She could have been a juvenile delinquent. No one should die like that."

"Agreed. And no one's death should be written off, either." I shook my head hard, anger erupting in me. "But Scott is done. We're done."

Zelda reached across and wrapped her arms around me. "Whatever is best." She patted my head soothingly.

Whatever had happened in our lives, Zelda and I would always have each other's back. We fell asleep curled under the blanket on the couch.

****

The next morning was rough. My eyes were crusty, and my mouth tasted like stale glue. I made waffles, bacon, and strong coffee. Zelda drenched her waffles in maple syrup and swiped her bacon through it. I drank one cup of strong coffee after another, relishing in the zing caffeine always brings to my system.

"What's our first move?" Zelda popped another slice of syrup dripping bacon into her mouth.

"Let's go talk with Celeste again," I said. "Find out what she's not telling anyone."

Zelda dressed in her clothes from the night before and took a rideshare back to her house. She promised to shower and change quickly. I would meet her at her house.

After a fast shower, I jumped into yoga pants and a sweater. The silence of the empty house weighed on me. My single status had never bothered me. I loved having my space and being able to do whatever I wanted whenever I wanted. I had never felt scared in my house before, and this new sensation was unpleasant. I made a mental note to stop by the electronics store today and pick up a home alarm system. The commercials made it look easy enough to install. I could get it done before bed tonight.

I drove to Zelda's house and let myself in. While I waited for her to get ready, I got a notebook out of my tote and made notes on what we learned so far. Doing it might spur us to discover a connection. Since it was a short list, it contained no surprises.

Zelda came downstairs in jeans and a fuzzy sweater. "Nate called while I was getting ready. He wants to go for lunch, but I'm pretty full from breakfast. I suggested an early dinner. Suppose we'll be done by then?"

"I can't imagine why not. We're just going to Celeste's. Shouldn't take long." I raised my notebook. "I've been jotting down notes on what we know so far. It'll help us find a link."

"Makes sense. I'll grab one and do the same. Then we can compare notes." She opened a drawer and tucked a small, shiny notebook into her purse. "Let's go."

After putting on a huge pair of sunglasses that covered most of her face, and we headed straight for Celeste's house, Zelda at the wheel. We debated about bringing more sweets but decided against it. If she hadn't taken her insulin, she might end up on the floor with a blood sugar in the dangerous range. I didn't want that on my conscience. We parked in the same place as before and walked up the front steps. The television was blaring loud, and I knocked hard enough to make the door shudder.

The television went silent, and the door opened. "Did you bring more maple bars?" Celeste asked, eyeing our empty hands.

"Did you dose for the one yesterday?" I replied.

She scoffed and eyed Zelda. "You're not supposed to talk about my medical conditions around other people."

"For heaven's sake, Miss Stewart," my best pal said. "Everyone in town knows you have diabetes. We've all watched you pass out at the holiday market after your second dozen cookies."

Celeste looked taken back. "For your information, the baker didn't properly inform me of the ingredients." She raised a hand to her chest in indignation. "Am I supposed to guess at how many carbs are in each cookie?"

I remembered she spent a week on my floor after the holiday market incident last year. She would have been better off guessing at the carbs than not taking any insulin "Celeste, after we spoke yesterday, we have a few more questions. Do you mind if we come in?"

She didn't look welcoming, but finally held the door open for us to enter. "Fine, but make it quick. My stories come on in thirty minutes."

I nodded, and we took the same seats as yesterday. "Celeste, you said you didn't notice anything the day the girl was attacked. Is that right?"

Celeste nodded.

"Is that what happened? Or did you notice something and get up to determine what it was? That's why you were at the back door by the time Neveah was running away. You saw something, too. Out the back." I motioned towards the back door in the kitchen. I let my words sit in the air.

Celeste gazed at her hands, making a close

examination of her cuticles. "What if I did?"

My breath caught in my throat.

"Miss Stewart, we don't want to get anyone in trouble or nothing." Zelda's voice cracked. "I was Buffy, the dead girl's, teacher. I need to learn what happened to her. Really happened." Zelda had actual tears in her eyes.

Celeste chewed a cuticle before answering. "I might have noticed something out there."

"What did you see?" I asked.

"I don't rightly know." She frowned and dropped her hand. "A growl?" She shook her head. "I realize it sounds crazy, but I heard a growl out there. Loud and deep."

I shook my head. "It doesn't sound crazy."

"I walked to the back door to investigate," she said. "That's when I noticed it."

"The animal?" Zelda asked.

Celeste shook her head. "It wasn't no animal. It ran like a man but was hairy as a beast. Don't think I've ever seen so much hair on a man and not a stitch of clothing."

My eyes widened. "He was nude?"

"I didn't see his dingle dangles, if that's what you're asking, but he didn't have any pants neither. That's why I didn't tell the police. It sounds crazy." She held up her hands in frustration. "I got enough problems without being called crazy, too."

"It doesn't sound crazy to us," I said. "You observed something you can't explain. I understand exactly how you'd feel."

Celeste nodded and wiped a hand across her eyes. "Thanks for not assuming I'm crazy."

"You're not crazy, Celeste." She was a lot of things, but not crazy. "You up on your meds and all?" I inquired, careful not to be specific.

"Yes, ma'am. I won't be visiting you anytime soon."

"Good. I'll hold you to that." Zelda and I stood and headed for the door. "You take care of yourself."

We exchanged goodbyes with Celeste and headed out to the car.

"So, if it walks like a werewolf and howls like a werewolf," Zelda contemplated as she slid the sunglasses on and pulled away from the curb.

I leaned back in the seat with a sigh. "Then it's a werewolf."

Chapter Twelve

As soon as we got back to Zelda's house, I picked up my car and headed for the nearest big box store. An employee from the electronics department got me set up and I was out of the store within an hour. The system was simple to install, and I felt handy doing it all myself. After I set up the account online, I'd be able to access the system from my phone. Zelda and my future alone looked bright. I took a quick circle of the mall and picked up a couple bath bombs and iced coffee as a special treat.

I hadn't missed a day of work in over two years and was tempted to call in sick for tomorrow. The sun was bright, and the trees were just losing their leaves. This time of year was my favorite, right before everything died and slept. I filled the tub with hot water and a bath bomb. The water immediately formed with rainbow colors and citrusy scent that soothed my soul. I decided right then I would not work tomorrow. Grabbing my cell phone, I followed the call off work automated system and received approval by the time the tub was full.

I sunk into the scalding water and sighed. My mind wandered through recent events. First, to the death of Buffy Stephens and then to my personal issues with Scott. Thinking of him made me groan but not in a sexy way. I never really felt we'd gotten past the early stages of a relationship. Previously, I chalked it up to our respective careers. Atherton was a small town, and Scott often wore more than the hat of a detective. He spoke at schools and community centers and coordinated neighborhood watch groups. I wasn't innocent in all this, lack of contribution to the relationship business. Long shifts at the hospital caused me to feel exhausted on my days off, both physically and emotionally. As my muscles relaxed, I wondered if there was something more that kept us the two of us stunted.

I sunk deeper into the water. Whatever kept us from moving forward, a break would be good for both of us. I dried off and slipped on my thread bare velour track and pulled my hair into a ponytail. I was sitting on the couch with my digital book reader when the alarm system alerted me to movement at the front door. I froze, unsure of what to do. No one knocked. I opened the app on my tablet and saw a person dressed in dark clothes wedge something in the door crack, then turn, and leave. I couldn't make out anything else about them. Not their height, weight or even the sex.

I turned off the alarm from my phone and carefully opened the door. A piece of notebook paper fluttered to the porch. I picked it up and unfolded it. In uneven block letters it read, "Dylan Condon." Nothing more. Tentatively, I stepped off the porch and took a quick look, up and down the street. A couple of houses down, kids played basketball in the front yard, but no strange cars or people.

I hurried inside and locked the door behind me. After grabbing my phone, I took a photo and sent it to Zelda.

—*look at this. WTF?*—

I went back to the couch, curled up and waited for a response. The phone pinged soon.

—Context?—

—Someone just put this in my door.—

I hit send and a moment later, the phone rang.

She didn't bother with pleasantries. "Seriously? Someone just put that in your front door? What the hell, Lex? I know I move on fast but you're not moving on from Scott already?"

"I couldn't make out who it was and when I walked outside, no one was around."

"Okay, are you familiar with this Dylan person?"

"No, I was hoping you were." Between the two of us, there were few people in town we couldn't didn't identify either by face or reputation.

The line was quiet for a moment before Zelda laughed long and loud. "Well shit. Of course! Almost forgot. I called him Condom in my head every time I saw his name. He took a creative writing class through adult education... maybe five years ago?" I heard her memory gears turn. "Anyway, good guy. Late twenties. Insanely creative, not great on time management."

"Why would someone put his name in my door?" I asked, more confused by the minute.

"Eh? No idea. I'm not sure if he graduated from high school. I don't remember having him in regular classes. Let me text a few of the other teachers and see what I can find out."

"Okay, let me know. How was your early dinner?

"Ugh. Nate's got a wicked sense of humor, but there's something off about him. Sometimes I can see it out of the corner of my eye."

Zelda usually noticed more about someone in the first few minutes of meeting them than others did over years. But I had to agree, there was something off about her boyfriend which I couldn't put a name to. "Besides the silk shirts?" I kept my tone neutral, but a tinge of humor leaked out.

Zelda laughed. "So, he's eccentric. That's not all bad. But it's not that. It's like he's distancing himself. I can't put my finger on it. I'll think about it later," she said with finality.

"You realize what they say about eccentrics? That's just crazy unless you're rich." I used my most disapproving tone, the one I reserved for patients who eat or drink when they've especially been told not to.

"Haha. You're funny. And not just funny looking, but funny." She hung up the phone, still laughing. It was a joke between us for decades and never failed to humor us.

Sitting the book aside, I pulled up an internet search on my phone and typed in the name written on the slip of paper. A social media page popped up. I clicked on it—and fell down into a rabbit hole of Dylan Condon's life. There were pictures of a bunch of costumes and theatrical makeup. Dylan apparently worked at a haunted house from August to early November every year. For the rest of the year, he worked at the local amusement park, operating a ride titled "Zambezi Zinger." It looked like some sort of roller coaster. The females in his photos looked were suspiciously young.

Like not of legal age young.

"Hmmm…. shady…" I said aloud and tucked myself deeper into my blankets. I put the phone aside and picked up the book. I attempted to get lost in the story, but my mind kept going back to Dylan's social media page.

"Shit."

I reached for the phone and opened the page again. It didn't take long to find a pattern. A cute young girl with him and a caption that alluded to being good friends. A few weeks later, a cryptic caption with a photo of the same girl and Dylan standing closer together. Another few weeks and his arm was draped around her shoulders, pulling her to his side, tight, like she was his possession. Most were blonde or light brunettes with long hair. Each one bore an uncomfortable resemblance to Buffy Stephens.

I immediately closed the app and texted Scott.

—*Did you investigate Dylan Condon?*—

I put my phone down, not expecting a response. When it rang, caller ID read Scott.

"Hello," I winced, remembering we ended on a rough note last night.

"What the hell did I tell you?" The force of his anger hit me across the line. "Look." He let out a dry, mean laugh. My heart sunk in my chest. "Leave it alone."

"I asked a simple question. Did you consider Dylan Condon for Buffy's murder or not?"

Silence held the line until Scott exhaled hard into the phone. "Yeah, yeah, I did. But he's got enough problems from us on other issues."

"He's into young girls, isn't he?" I tried to keep the excitement out of my voice. We were on to something. I could feel it.

"And you have that information? How?" Scott asked, surprised.

"Someone slipped a note with his name on it in my door tonight. I looked him up on social media and saw some questionable pictures." I left the door open for Scott to confirm my suspicions.

"I can't tell you anything on an open investigation, but you're not stupid. That's why I want you to stay out of it. Look, this is a small town and rocking the boat too much doesn't end well."

"So, you'd rather not rock the boat?" The picture of Buffy on the metal slab filled my vision. "Who are you protecting? I hope to heaven it's not her killer or a pedophile."

"Look, Lex. This has nothing to do with protecting anyone." A groan escaped him. "Dylan Condon is under investigation for indecent liberties with a minor. Several minors. The Chief wants him on that."

"But he was a suspect for Buffy's murder?" I asked, on the edge of my seat.

Silence again. I looked at the phone display to make sure he was still on the line.

"He was," Scott finally said, resignation in his voice. "He had interviewed Buffy that same day for a job at the haunted house. He was one of the last people to see her alive and, with his issues with young females, he was a viable suspect."

"Why can't he be good for both? Can't you charge him with different crimes?"

"Because… one of the girls whom we're investigating on the other charges, has a mom who is rich and powerful. Someone who, when she walks into the police department, everyone stands. The Chief wants Condon on those charges, not the homicide—murder—shit—the accident." He sighed hard again. "You're not making this easy, Lex."

"Buffy's death doesn't matter because some rich and powerful dick wants Dylan's ass?" I wasn't naïve I knew there were carefully defined social classes in

Atherton but the fact that the police department would be swayed by money surprised me.

"I've said too much, Lex." He sighed again. "Just promise me you'll stay out of this. I want to have a job and I don't want you getting caught up in anything."

Hysteria rose in my voice. "Is this how this town works?"

"That's how it always works everywhere, honey. The powerful get what they want and the rest of us just get by." He sounded tired and run down. "Look, I'm bushed. Let's cool down and talk in a few days, all right?"

My heart still skipped beats and bounced around my chest. "Fine." I smashed my finger on the end call buttoned with little satisfaction.

Confused, I fell back on the sofa. Had I been so stupid? There was more going on in this town than I'd considered. The world that Scott explained wasn't the one I grew up in—or I believed I lived in now. I racked my brain for hints and shook my head. I didn't have a Polly Anna world view, but was it possible I ignored the truth?

No number of blankets would keep me warm tonight. The chill came from inside.

Chapter Thirteen

I woke to my teeth vibrating from a blaring noise. I was scanning my bedroom for the source when Zelda threw open the door. Her mouth moved, but nothing came out. I fumbled for my phone and turned off the alarm. The silence was almost as deafening as the alarm.

Zelda rubbed her ears and dropped on the bed at my feet. "What was that?"

"Forgot to tell you, I installed a home alarm system yesterday. "I didn't get the notification that you were at the door. Sorry. I'll get you a code so you can come and go." I dropped back on the bed, numb and more exhausted than when I fell into bed last night.

Zelda shrugged. "Whatever works for you. You know I have this whole place warded. That reminds me, when we go visit your mama's house in Florida, I'll need to ward it. You have a camera we can use for them, too?"

After a few cool fall days, sunny Florida sounded perfect. Although I'm not sure how my parent's neighbors would take to Zelda burying things in the yard. I curled up hugging my pillow.

"Did you get anything on whomever left the note last night?" she asked.

"Nope, they kept their head down."

Zelda laid back next to me and crossed her hands under the back of her head. "It's like they knew you had a camera." Her voice trailed off. "But how would anyone know that? I didn't know it and I know everything."

I threw the blankets back and walked to the bathroom, leaving the door open a crack to talk. "Many people have them. They could have been playing it safe and assuming." Shivers coursed through me at the other possibility, that someone had watched me install it.

"That's true. You're not going to work today?"

"I called in yesterday and now I'm not feeling great. It's probably best to stay home and chill for the day." That was code when one of us wanted alone time.

"Uh huh. I got a sub for today. I did some calls on your Dylan Condon last night."

My time alone would have to wait. At least until we found Buffy's killer.

After I flushed the toilet and washed my hands, I quickly snuggled back into the bed. "I found some stuff out, too. You go first."

Zelda stared at the ceiling. "Nate works at the haunted house with him. He said Dylan pays special attention to young girls."

"Scott said something similar. How about we go pay him a visit?"

"Wait, wait." Zelda propped herself up on her elbow. "You talked to Scott? How did it go?"

I didn't meet her gaze. "It was okay. We agreed to meet in a few days." Rarely did I keep secrets from Zelda. In fact, I could count how many on both hands over the decades. I jumped out of bed and stumbled back to the bathroom. Turning on the water, I splashed my face.

"Okay, I'll wait downstairs for you," Zelda shouted over the water. The bedroom door closed. I jumped in the shower and soaped up quickly and saved washing my hair for another day.

Downstairs, Zelda had eggs and toast waiting. A tinge of guilt made me want to tell her everything that Scott said. Instead, I shoved eggs in my mouth. "Thanks for breakfast," I said through a mouthful of toast.

"You're welcome. I think Dylan lives in an apartment on the west side. You remember those old high rises?"

I frowned. "I thought those were for old folks."

Years earlier, the town fathers hoped the urban sprawl from Kansas City would reach Atherton and had constructed three apartment buildings, each five stories. At the time they were billed as state of the art, luxury high rise living. Few people took the builders up on the offer and those that did were mostly senior citizens. It quickly became known as the senior high rises.

Zelda shook her head. "Nope, anyone can live there, but they prefer seniors." She rolled her eyes. "We're not that far from them."

I stared at my plate and cringed at the idea in twenty years I could be one of the residents. "Right. Do you ever worry about growing old?"

Zelda stopped cleaning the skillet and stared out the window. "Don't be with Scott just to be with someone. And to answer your question, sure. I worry about it. But I have money set aside for the retirement home that goes on day trips to the casinos." She shrugged. "It's part of life. The cycle of nature. And with age comes wisdom, I hope. I'd rather grow old than the other option."

I agreed and finished my breakfast. Talking to Zelda which was usually flavored with four-letter words, always gave me a good perspective. We got in my car and drove across town. The westside featured a factory, warehouses, and the occasional office building. The apartment building sat up the hill from the haunted houses that clustered under the Twelfth Street bridge. It wasn't a comfortable place to live, more of a place to stay for a while.

The high-rise Dylan lived in looked like it was last updated in the 1970s. Large windows and aged and dented metal accents decorated the main floor. We parked out front and walked to the entrance. Inside, it was a controlled entry building.

"Hmm... you don't notice many of those in town," Zelda commented. "Wonder how we'll get in."

I eyed the keypad for a minute and typed in a series of numbers. The door magically buzzed. She raised an eyebrow.

"My college dorm had the same system. It had a master code that would unlock it." I held the door open for Zelda.

She winked. "And why anyone trusted you as the Dorm Manager I will never know."

"Hey, I was trustworthy."

"Uh, hu. He lives on the fifth floor," she said and pushed the up button on the elevator, after we entered the compartment.

"Any idea which apartment?" I asked. "And how did you find out all of this?"

On the fifth floor, Zelda walked out of the elevator and glanced up and down the hall. "Not a hundred percent sure. Nate said we'd find it by odor. He is useful on occasion." She crept down the hallway, sniffing.

I followed behind, hoping no one noticed us. Zelda looked like a child hunting witch, sniffing the air as she went. At the end of the hall, the scent of skunk wafted from the last unit. I wrinkled my nose.

"Bingo," Zelda said, "He must have some good stuff. No sticks and leaves for Dylan." She pounded on the door, waited a moment, and pounded again. She leaned her head against the door and held her hands against it.

"Nothing. Not even a television." She frowned. "What pothead doesn't at least have the television going?" Her hand reached for the doorknob, and it turned. I nodded in agreement. Eyebrows raised, she opened the door.

The door opened to a small, spotless kitchen with a jar of peanut butter and a loaf of bread on the counter. Two steps into the apartment, we saw a living room that barely fit a sagging couch and monster television. A small bedroom and bathroom sat off to the right. The entire apartment couldn't have been over four hundred square feet. One wall featured photos of Dylan in various costumes. They were the only personal items in the apartment. It made me sad to think the man had lived there for years and that's all he had. Perhaps that's all he wanted.

"Hmm… doesn't seem like much of anything," Zelda said, hands on her hips. "Vibe isn't horrible, just muddy. He's not what I would call a clean soul. Dude smokes so much weed I am getting high from breathing, so there's that."

"Right. Who has a clean soul at this point? Should we go through the closets?"

"Eh, I don't think so. Seems invasive."

I chuckled. "But breaking into his apartment isn't?"

She held up her hands in defense. "Hey, I just turned the knob. The rest happened on its own."

"Okay, let's go through a couple of things and get out of here."

We divided up. I headed to the bedroom to examine the closet. It held costumes, jeans, hoodies, and T-shirts. Shoes on the bottom. The bathroom held even less. Antiperspirant, electric razor, and a collection of cologne. Massive collections of cologne. I sniffed one and grimaced. If that's what others considered sexy, I'll pass.

Zelda stood in the small foyer. "Kitchen's done. Nothing but chips and crackers and cookies. Stoner food."

"Nothing in here but half of a department store's cologne section." I waved a hand in front of my face and joined Zelda. "Let's get out of here. He could be down at the haunted house."

"That makes sense." We walked back into the hall and closed the door. "Should we lock the door?"

I shrugged. "Let's not. What if he doesn't have a key?"

We took the elevator downstairs and pointed the car down the hill towards the Twelfth Street viaduct to check out the different haunted houses. Most were old warehouses whose owners had converted parts of the buildings into haunted houses for the holiday season.

I parked in front of one that had a neon sign that read, "Demon's Lair" with dripping blood drops on each side. "Classy," I said, oozing sarcasm.

"It might look better lit up?" Zelda stared at it, frowning. "Let's see if anyone is here."

She walked to the metal main door, a holdover from whatever the building had been previously. "I'm gonna try my luck again." She reached for the door, pulled, and found it locked. "Damn." Balling a fist, she banged on the door. The door didn't rattle or move.

I looked around the street at the other buildings. They all appeared empty with no cars out front. "I don't think these places wake until closer to dark."

Zelda sighed. "You're right." She turned back to the car, and we got in. "What next?"

I started the car and pulled back onto Twelfth Street. "Let's grab lunch and go over our notes." We drove up Twelfth Street past Dylan's apartment building. I almost wrecked the car when I saw the street lined on both sides with police cars, their lights flashing.

"Oh shit!" I screamed and jerked the car to the curb. "Did you see that, Zel?"

Her neck was twisted around to get a better view of the scene and a hand on the door. She turned back to me. "Yeah, what are the chances that's not connected to us?"

Chapter Fourteen

"Under normal circumstances, I'd say zero. Considering recent events, I'm going to say ninety-five to, ninety-nine percent."

"What do we do?" Her hand remained on the door handle. She was ready to run.

I stared at the steering wheel. "We can't go over there, can we?" My breath caught in my chest. Zelda exhaled hard.

"No." She held up her hands. "Best to stay away. Let's eat. We'll feel better after we eat. And I'll feel better after I find a bathroom. My bladder isn't what it used to be."

I drove across town to a local bar and grill that had the best fried pickles in town. We slid into a booth in the back. I ordered a diet soda, and Zelda ordered her usual margarita. Instead of entrees, we ordered a bunch of appetizers to share.

The food came out hot and fast and Zelda popped a fried pickle in her mouth. Her lips made an O shape, and she breathed in and out to cool it off. I dipped a hunk of bread in hummus and ate it. My phone buzzed. Three messages from Scott. The instant knot in my stomach told me the messages were about whatever had happened at Dylan's apartment.

"What is it?" Zelda said around a mouth of food.

"Some texts from Scott. I'm ignoring them." I

dropped my phone back in my bag and moved in for the plate of buffalo fries, savoring the tangy sauce and blue cheese.

Zelda nodded. "Probably for the best. You know I was hoping for more interesting stuff today. Not that we haven't had enough lately, but this Dylan guy seems really shady."

"It appears his connections to Buffy are slim. Perhaps the case is better for the sex crimes thing."

"What sex crimes?" Her eyes went as big as hubcaps. "Why am I just hearing about this?"

I forgot I wasn't supposed to say anything and strived to keep my tone neutral. "Scott told me last night that the police want Dylan on sex crimes. There's more evidence against him there than with Buffy's murder. Plus, they're getting pressure from the community."

Zelda rolled her eyes. "Honey, I've been a teacher here for two decades. I understand that code. What you mean to say is some rich and or influential parent's kid is involved and making a stink with the department. Hell, probably the whole municipal system." She dipped a fried pickle in ranch and chewed.

"You know about this?" We had never discussed this, and I thought we talked about everything.

Zelda reached for a mozzarella stick, broke it in half, pulling the hot cheese apart. "People have been throwing around their money, last names and reputations, for as long as I can remember. It's gotten worse since more people have relocated here to get out of the city. Like I'm supposed to know or care who they are. I don't agree with it. Might be one of the reasons I consider leaving the teaching field on a regular basis. But it happens, everywhere. Atherton isn't special in that."

I stared down at the table of fried goodness. Suddenly, not as hungry as I was before. "It's been a surprise for me."

"Of course it has, no one tries to bully a nurse by throwing their money around. never comes out in their favor so consider yourself lucky. You're one of the few professions in this town that is still respected." She winked and I did feel better. "Let's go over the notes and see if we missed anything."

We spent the rest of the time going over notes and chowing down on fat and salt. There were no other clues or points we could come up with. With our bellies full, we piled back in the car and headed to my house. Our spirits were down, and we'd even tossed around the idea of giving up and going back to our normal, boring jobs— but only for a split second. There was no way we would let Buffy's death go unanswered.

As I pulled into the driveway I saw Scott sitting on the front steps. His face looked twisted and dark. Last time I saw him looking that grim, he'd suggested we move in together and I shot it down. This stare had nothing to do with our relationship, but I wished it did.

"That doesn't look good," I said.

"Yeah, I'm gonna head home." Zelda was out the door and on the way to her car before I shifted into Park.

I took a deep breath as I got out of the car.

"I'm going to need to see both of you inside," Scott shouted after Zelda, a heavy edge of irritation in his voice. "Now."

She stalked toward me, cursing under her breath. She stopped, planted her fists on her hips, and gave Scott a look that often wilted weaker men. "What exactly do you want with me?"

He stretched to his full height and adjusted his belt at the waistband. "Let's talk about catching the two of you on a surveillance camera, breaking and entering." He turned and walked up the steps, opening the door for us.

I grimaced and cursed when the alarm started beeping. "Stop, I installed an alarm." I hurried up behind him with Zelda on my heels.

He laughed. "You had an alarm installed? That's rich."

I bit my tongue and entered the code on the keypad before dropping my tote. "What are—" I started.

He moved fast to get in my face. "You shut up."

Zelda pushed between us like lightning. "Oh hell no."

Scott shoved her aside. "Both of you, shut up. I don't know where to start." He shook his head. "Look, I told you to stay out of it, didn't I? I told you to leave it alone, right?"

Half in shock, I nodded. His anger frightened me. Zelda's fists were balled at her side and her face blotchy red.

"And yet you, both of you, ran ahead and did the exact opposite of what I told you to do. And not only that, but you also got caught on a damn surveillance camera." He threw his arms up in the air, pacing the living room.

"Where was the camera?" Zelda asked.

"That's what you ask?" Scott's face flushed and each word spit out. "Management had it installed after a bunch of break-ins. We moved to arrest Dylan, found the door unlocked, and pulled the video. The Chief wants me to bring you both in."

"What?" I had never been arrested or even came

close to such a momentous event in my entire forty-plus years. Had I technically committed a crime? Yes, but it wasn't like we had intent.

Scott's gaze bore into me. "Let me reiterate. Both of you were caught on camera, breaking and entering. And the Chief wants someone's head." He eyed both of us. "Guess you can decide between the two of you. It doesn't matter to me. I have to bring someone in. Hell, one or both, doesn't matter to me."

I held the door open for him. "Wait outside."

"This ain't my first time around the block, sweetheart. I'm not leaving without someone in handcuffs."

"And this is my home. And you don't have a warrant." My anger rose. "Or you would have already pulled it out for us to admire."

"I have probable cause," he spit back. "And I'm already here." He waved his arms around. "I can do whatever I want."

He wasn't backing down. Neither was I. My knuckles turned white in the tight grip on the doorknob.

Again, Zelda stepped between us. "Stop it. Just stop." Her breathing was heavy. "I'll go with you, Scott." She dropped her hands. "As long as you don't whip out your dick to show me what a man you are. You've already done that enough."

I wasn't sure how school administrators viewed one of their teachers getting arrested, but imagined it wasn't good. "Zel, you can't. What will happen to your classroom?" For years the school board had had put up with her being detained for protest marches, but this was more than her running her mouth over social or political issues.

Her chin raised, eyes on fire, chest jutted out. Her try me pose. "I've got twenty years in as of last week so. F it. They don't like it, I can retire." She threw a look to kill gaze to Scott. "Might be I'll start a life of crime. And what's the penalty for assaulting an officer? Might want to handcuff me before I do."

A wry smile broke out on Scott's face. "Well, you're too late for whoring." He reached for Zelda's arm. "Let's get a move on." There was never any love lost between them, but his comment was beyond the pale.

"I'll be down to get you out in a bit," I said.

"Don't show up for a while. The Chief may get the idea to book both of you." Scott pulled a set of handcuffs from his waistband. "Then who will bail your asses out?"

Zelda held out her arm to him and he clicked the cuffs into place. She turned to me. "Don't worry about me, Lex. I can handle this asshole." She threw me a wink over her shoulder as she walked with Scott to the unmarked police car at the curb.

Chapter Fifteen

Grim expression on his face, Scott pulled away from the curb while Zelda's mouth moved a mile a minute from the back seat. He'd likely regret arresting her before they made it out of my neighborhood.

Zelda could hold her own with the best of them. I shouldn't be worried about her, but this situation was turning toward a dangerous, and uncomfortable, direction.

I closed the door and grabbed a glass of water, savoring my options. First thing, I would take Scott's advice and give it time before I went to the jail to bail Zelda out. I sat on the couch and propped up my feet to consider those options.

What evidence did I have that Dylan Condon was the killer? Suspicion and a note on my door wasn't much, really. Sure, he was shady and weird, and harbored an abnormal attraction for young girls, but that doesn't make him a killer. A sick fuck more like it. I closed my eyes, pondering the next clue. What was the motivation behind someone put the note in my door? Was it a red herring, meant to led Zelda and me into trouble?

Who might be capable of Buffy's murder if not her abuser? After Zelda talked to Buffy's friends at school, she came away none of them had the guts for a crime of that level. No, it had to be an adult. Someone physically strong. It might be a woman. Early in my nursing career,

I'd spent time in an inner city Emergency Room and witnessed the damage some women can inflict when they're pushed. Anyone who said men were the more dangerous sex had never seen a woman rip out a guy's eyeballs with her bare hands and leave the flesh on his face shredded.

But what woman had the motive or amount of anger necessary to do something like that to a kid? How many enemies did a fourteen-year-old have? No, this was a crime of passion, not an accident or a random attack. The murderer knew Buffy. Catching her there at the right time, alone. What was done required a certain degree of planning.

Standing, I grabbed my tote then headed out the door, making sure to set the alarm as I left. I needed to talk to the one person Zelda and I had yet to get to yet Buffy's mom.

I exhaled hard and pulled up the local newspaper on my phone once I got in the car. There should have been time for the obituary to be published. Scrolling, I found it painfully short. She loved movies, especially horror. She enjoyed movie marathons and making movies on her cell phone. She had wanted to do special effects makeup for movies after high school. Tears rose from the corner of my eyes. The girl had barely experienced life. Her mother and a younger sister survived her. My heart broke for the sister. In a small town like Atherton, she'll never get away from being *"the one whose sister was murdered."* The obit stated visitation was scheduled for tomorrow with the funeral to be held on Wednesday morning. It also gave her mother's full name.

A people search showed only one listing for a Marie Stephens. I plugged the address in to the maps app before

I pulled out of the driveway. I didn't have the words to say to Buffy's mom, but I'd use all the skills I'd learned for dealing with traumatized patients so I felt sure they would come. I had to find out who had been paying Buffy attention lately. That might lead to the killer.

The Stephens' house sat one street over from Neveah's. It seemed strange that the two girls didn't know each other, but the age difference might explain that. I didn't recognize most of the people that graduated over two grades ahead of me in high school. Things probably had changed little, even if it had been over twenty years.

I parked a few houses down and turned off the engine. What would I say? "Hi, I'm a nurse at the local hospital and I don't think an animal killed your daughter." I sighed and got out, walking to the front of the house. The words would come.

The front yard had been mowed short at the end of the season. The mulch from the flower beds had all washed away in the rains earlier in the year, lonely bits of wood and dried up plants and strangled weeds littered the path. The front porch creaked beneath my feet but held solid. Paint peeled along the shutters and screen door.

I rang the doorbell twice in quick succession and waited. After two minutes, I opened the screen door and knocked hard. I waited another three minutes. Deep in the house, the sound of a tea kettle screamed. A woman with blonde hair streaked with dark lowlights opened the door. Her eyes were red and blood shot; her face carried that dull, placid look of a person struggling to cope and having nowhere to turn.

"Can I help you?" she asked, her voice rough and

quiet.

"I'm Lexi Burns. I work at the hospital, and I…" The words died in my throat. Tears sprung at the corner of my eyes.

The woman nodded and pushed the screen door open. "You tried to save my girl, didn't ya?"

The knot still in my throat, I nodded. "I'm so very sorry for your loss, Ms. Stephens."

"Come on in. You want a cup of tea?" She held the door open, and I followed her into the small, dark house. "Or maybe something stronger," she said over her shoulder as she headed to the small kitchen, leaving me at the door.

"Thank you. But you don't have to do that. I came to pay my respects, Ms. Stephens. I wanted to tell you we did everything possible." I almost believed the words.

She waved her hand at me. "I saw you did. I'm a medical assistant in the rehab unit next door." She got two cups out and dropped a tea bag in each and filled them with hot water from the kettle. From the cabinet above the stove, she pulled out a small bottle of whiskey, mostly full, and poured a nip in each teacup. "I had come over with another girl to get lunch." She shrugged. "So, I just happened to be walking back when I got the call." Her voice carried no inflection. I recognized a lack of sleep from the tremor in her hands.

"There's some meds you can take," I said as I took the teacup from her. As soon as the words came out, I realized how heartless they sounded.

Marie smiled. "Already got them." She raised the teacup and sipped. "Figure I'd save them for tomorrow." She motioned for me to follow her into the small living room. We took seats next to each other on the small couch. We sat in silence for a while, sipping our tea.

"May I ask you a few questions about Buffy?" I put my cup on the coffee table. The nip of whiskey warmed me from the inside out.

Marie nodded and took another sip of hers.

I cleared my throat and said, "Did Buffy have... bad words with anyone?" I couldn't bring myself to say enemies. A child didn't have enemies.

Marie sat her cup down and folded her hands in her lap. Knowing eyes returned my gaze. "You don't think what happened was an accident either, do you?"

I took a deep breath before answering. "No, Marie, I don't," I held my hands out to hers. "I want to help and get to the truth." The words seemed small.

Marie leaned back on the sofa, sinking into the threadbare cushions. She looked small and fragile. "As soon as the police told me an animal attacked my girl, I didn't believe them. I even asked the coroner, but he blew me off. I'm just a medical assistant." Tears flowed down her cheeks.

Neveah's words came to mind. No one believed her either. This time, I took her hand. "Marie, you're a mother. That overrides everything." I squeezed her fingers. She nodded and wiped the tears from her face. "Tell be about your girl."

A smile brightened her face. "So wonderful. Smart, pretty, kind. A real good kid. She watched her little sister and never objected. Didn't complain when we didn't have money for things she wanted or special activities." She shook her head. "That girl never grumbled. She loved movies. She even made a couple of movies on her phone." The tears flowed between each word.

Something inside my brain perked. Would it be

possible Buffy was making a movie just before the attack? Might she have caught her killer on the camera? "Did she have her phone wither that day?"

Marie frowned. "I haven't seen it. I'd love to have it though. There are some photos on there of the family. She did a nice film for our family reunion this summer."

"Double check with the police. I would ask them myself but I'm not in their good graces right now."

Unexpectedly, my phone dinged with a text notification. It was from Zelda.

—These fools say I'm free to go. Want to come get me?—

Time to spring Zelda from jail. "I'm sorry, Ms. Stephens, I've got to leave."

Hope lit Marie's face and the shreds of death parted. "You're investigating my daughter's death, aren't you? You'll find the killer?"

"I shouldn't be." I shook my head. "I shouldn't be involved. I'm only a nurse. But I want to find the truth, and the only way I can do it is to find it myself." I stood and moved to the door. "I'll let you know if I find anything."

Marie followed. At the door, she wrapped me in a tight hug. I hugged her back just as tight. She smelled like soap and whiskey, and it broke my heart.

Chapter Sixteen

The moment I pulled into a parking space in front of the police station, exhaustion washed over me. Crime fighting should be left to the younger crowd. To people with faster brain synapses and more flexible hip joints. My shoulder strained when I pulled the heavy door open to the police station.

A tired-looking man sat at the desk. His name tag said Nakamura. No way this was a relation to the coroner. But in these parts, it wasn't a common name.

"Can I help you?" He sounded as tired as he looked.

"Yes, I'm here for Zelda Allen." After no sign of recognition from the desk sergeant, I continued. "Detective Devlin brought her in earlier for breaking and entering."

"Oh yeah, she was my English teacher in tenth grade," he answered. "Who knew she was a criminal at heart?"

My hackles rose. "I believe she is innocent until proven guilty in a court of law." At least that's what the introduction to one of my favorite TV shows always said. I'm not sure if that's legit law or not.

"Whatever, lady. Have a seat, and I'll let Devlin know you're here."

I went to take a seat and turned back to the officer. "One quick question, are you related to the coroner?"

His eyes wrinkled beneath his frown. "Why?

Because we're both Asian?"

My eyebrows raised as I pointed to his name plaque. "Because you both have the same last name?"

He waved a dismissive hand. "Oh that. Yeah, he's my dad."

I nodded. So, I wasn't a racist. I wanted to point that out but didn't. "And you didn't follow in his footsteps?"

His face lit up. "Nope, Dad got me the job here. My sister did though, first in her class at the University of Missouri - Kansas City. She'll be here practicing in no time."

As proud as the man looked, I'm guessing he didn't understand nepotism, or didn't care. "How lucky for you." I took the seat in the hard plastic chair across from his desk.

He left the desk for a few moments and came back looking grim and overly law enforcement. Scott must have informed him who I was. "He'll be out in a minute."

"And Zelda?"

He either didn't hear me or pretended not to because he didn't respond. He shuffled papers and studied them hard. What if they kept her? Could they do that? She said they were done with her, but were they? My watch said it was almost five o'clock, the end of business day. What if Zelda needed an attorney? Where would I find an available lawyer at this time of night? Especially one who knows their ass from their elbow? I fidgeted with the strap of my bag and the neckline of my sweater and wished for someone like Ben Matlock.

The door opened and Scott stood in the doorway, the creases still visible in his plaid shirt. In my peripheral vision, I saw the desk cop staring. Whatever was said between us would be repeated back to anyone and everyone later whether they cared or not.

"Miss Burns, come on back." Scott's voice was tired and tight. I hung back as he walked through the station and to his corner office. In no way did I want to come across as confrontational. At least not right now. Zelda sat in the chair across from Scott's desk, handcuffs in her lap and her face tired. She gave me a smile as I walked in. I hurried across the room and wrapped my arms around her.

"No touching the prisoner," Scott said as he closed the office door.

I turned to blast him with anger but stopped when I saw his smug expression. He wanted to rile me. I wasn't going to give him the pleasure. I took a seat next to Zelda and folded my hands in my lap. And waited.

Scott smirked as he took a seat at the desk. "I've briefed Ms. Allen on the situation and thought it best if I filled you in, as well." He shuffled the short pile of papers in front of him. "We have you on video breaking into Dylan Condon's apartment. Now, that's an issue in and of itself." He glared at Zelda. "Miss Allen and I have been discussing what occurred and your involvement. Even though the video clearly shows both of you going in, she is adamant she entered alone." Frustration oozed from each word.

I didn't need to glance at Zelda to see the huge grin on her face.

"Here's where it gets interesting." Scott stopped and waited for my reaction. "Dylan is missing,"

I willed my face to freeze. Was that why Dylan's apartment looked so clean and empty? Could he have skipped town or was someone there before us? If so, why didn't the cameras catch them?

Scott continued. "The two of you meddling have caused the shit to hit the fan here and at the District Attorney's office. I told you the Chief wanted him—Dylan, not the DA—for the sex crimes, not murder. Now he's missing and half the people in this town are breathing down our necks."

"How is this my problem?" I gestured to Zelda. "Or our problem?"

She held up her cuffed hands. "Wait for it; he's getting there."

"You've already listened to this?" I asked.

She nodded. "The rough draft version. I'm enjoying the finished version now." She turned to Scott. "Your delivery adds an intensity that is very engaging." It was like she was critiquing a student's performance.

Scott's gaze narrowed, and he seethed in her general direction. "As I was saying, you've both messed this up."

Zelda rolled her eyes. "Can you get to the point? I'm hungry and have to pee again." She held up the cuffs. "All the women officers are off today. These guys hate it when I have to pee," she whispered conspiratorially toward me.

I suppressed a laugh that would be disastrous in this situation, but I learned from a recent road trip exactly how often Zelda had to pee. It was on average every forty-five minutes, fifteen if she chugged liquid like she had at lunch. These guys must be annoyed indeed.

Scott squeezed his eyes closed in frustration. "Right. Look, we're letting you go as long as both of you don't leave the area and stay out of crime fighting for good. Stop messing around. Go back to your jobs and whatever lives you have and give up the pretend sleuthing."

That was a direct dig at me. Scott had complained

many times I didn't have a life because I enjoyed things he didn't and didn't pretend to like the things he did. I went to a baseball game a time or two but is it really necessary to go to every game and watch them all the time on the television? I thought not. Give me a good documentary or book any day.

"We can stay out of the way. Will she be charged?"

Scott was a master at leaving important details out. I wanted to make sure we understood things.

He grimaced. "That's up in the air. It's always a possibility until the statute of limitations expires." He counted on his fingers while doing hard math. "That's another ten years in this state."

Zelda rolled her eyes. "Great, about the same time I get my AARP card." She held up her hands again. "Let's get these off and get rolling before I curse you into next year. I'm over you."

Zelda's "I'm over you" usually came right before she lost her shit. We stood and Scott remained behind the desk until the weight of our glare got him up. He slowly fished in his pockets for the key and finally found it, unlocking Zelda's wrists.

She didn't give him the satisfaction of rubbing her wrists or showing discomfort. But I saw the red marks of irritation. My anger rose. He didn't have to hurt or handcuff her. Where was she going to run? She'd taught over half the town at one point or another. They could identify her before she got to the city limits.

"My purse?" she asked.

"Out at the front with Nakamura." Scott dropped on the chair and motioned to the door without looking up, his attention on the paperwork on the desk.

"Nakamura?" Zelda gazed at me, eyebrows raised.

I nodded. "We'll talk about it later."

Scott didn't glance up from the papers on the desk. "No, you won't. I said stay out of it."

Zelda rolled her eyes again. She grabbed my arm and pushed me out the door. "Let's get out of here before both of us end up behind bars."

Nakamura took his time getting Zelda's personal effects. Each item from the purse had to be cataloged and checked back out. She was fond of lip products and the list was long. Heaven help the man if her lip butter was missing.

They put everything back in its place and we headed out. We didn't say a word until we got into the car, started it, and had an eighties hair band blaring.

Zelda stared straight ahead when she spoke. "That sumbitch is going to pay, Lex. I will gut him and use 'em for bait."

It wasn't Zelda's voice. She was channeling her Grandma Francis. The woman died when we were kids. Grandma Francis had put the fear of God in most of the town and had probably roughed up the rest. She owned the one bar in town and didn't need a bouncer. But she made the prettiest quilts and the best mackerel cakes and fried potatoes I'd ever had. I still had one of her quilts in a closet upstairs.

"Uh huh," I said agreeably. You didn't mess with Zelda when the Grandma Francis' voice came out. Zel's mom had done her best to get that side of the family out of her, but the older Zelda got, the more it showed. "Let's get you home and comfortable."

She shook her head. "I'm not eighty. I need a toilet, a beer, and some food." Her face twisted up in disgust. "Would you believe they tried to serve me donuts?

You've experienced what that does to my system. I'd blown up that toilet and then they'd blamed me when it stopped up."

I resisted the urge to laugh again. There was no talking or reasoning with Zelda in this mood. "All right let's get you home and you can get a beer and pee. At the same time, even."

Zelda sniffed her armpit. "Eh, might take a bath with that beer. The jail scent is all over me."

I agreed the jail carried had a certain smell, like a combination of burnt coffee, commercial disinfectant, and body odor. I couldn't detect any of it on Zelda, but I didn't want to contradict her in her current state.

At Zelda's house, I got her in a hot bath with a cold beer. I ordered meal delivery from a chicken place and started her laundry. There were no rules saying I couldn't help my bestie in a time of need. After all, she would take the criminal charge for me.

The food arrived, and I set it up on the kitchen table. Instead of eating out of the containers I pulled out Zelda's plates, glasses, and silverware. Real plates seemed less sad.

Zelda came down the hall at the same time I finished. Her face was flushed from the hot water and the alcohol. She was wrapped in a fuzzy red robe I'd bought her a few years ago. Plopping on the dining room chair, she drained the rest of her beer, and I handed her another.

"Thanks for this," she said as she speared a piece of chicken with her fork and popped it in her mouth. "I didn't realize how hungry I was until I got out of the bath."

"No worries, I started your laundry, too." I stuck a French fry into my mouth. "No reason to have you looking half- assed going into work," I said with a smile.

Zelda put down her fork and held her hands in a prayer position in front of her. "Thank you, my love! I don't know what I'd do without you." She nodded her head. "Probably end up in a ditch somewhere."

I finished chewing my bite of chicken and answered. "Or prison."

We both laughed. It was good to share a moment with my oldest friend. Over dinner, I caught Zelda up on my visit to Buffy's mom. Here I believed my sleepy little town was just that. Instead, it's a hotbed of corruption and nepotism.

Chapter Seventeen

The next day I texted Zelda a "I hate mornings" cartoon to make sure she was up. When she liked the message five minutes later, I finished getting ready for work. Nothing phased her for too long.

After lunch, I settled into charting on one of my patients when the results from admissions lab work came back. I groaned and dropped my head back. Nakamura was the patient's doctor. My theory was his patients usually didn't make it up to my floor.

"Looks like Lexi won the lottery today!" Tracey said, a bit too enthusiastically. "You're paging Nakamura, aren't you?"

While all the doctors were too good or too talented for Tracey to verbally disembowel, I held no such reservations but any interaction with Nakamura would push the limits of my agreement with Scott. Compliance was tenuous, and I wasn't going to waste breaking it on a physician who should have retired sometime during the last century.

I groaned again and nodded. Laughter erupted through the unit, and I resisted the urge to throw a stapler at them. "He's coming down here and you realize he's going to start something. It's in the air today." Tracey smacked her hands together loudly. "And I got a front-row seat." She leaned her chair back and took a swig out of her cup, a huge grin on her face.

I stuck my tongue at her and paged Nakamura, my heart racing. I went about the rest of my charting and waited for him.

Ten minutes later, a tall, slender man with salt and pepper hair appeared across the counter from me. His face was creased in a disapproving frown and his hands were shoved deep into the wide pockets of his white lab coat.

I sensed his harden stare boring through me. He cleared his throat, loud and prolonged, like a toad was lodged there. I took an extra minute to review my charting and calm my nerves, hit save, and leaned back in the chair before acknowledging him.

"Can I help you?" I said, in my friendliest voice. I would have sworn I heard Tracey make a 'ooh' sound behind me. Heat rose in my face, and I willed it down.

The frown never left his face. "Nakamura. You paged me? To the unit?" His voice oozed contempt.

I returned his frown. "No, I paged you to sign off on a script. You didn't need to come down. I sent it down to the pharmacy so if you'll just sign off on it— "

Nakamura folded his arms across his chest. "I just need to sign off. That's it?" he asked, contempt obvious. "You now have M.D. behind your name?"

I lifted one eyebrow. "It's simple." I didn't say he was stupid, but it was heavily implied. "A standard script for the patient's condition." My hand wandered to the hem of my scrub and played with the stitching.

"Standard script for the condition?" He repeated the words with a question in each syllable.

I'd dealt with enough doctors in various forms over the years. There was little any of them could do to truly annoy me but I still disliked confrontation in any form.

Acting holier than thou and delaying a simple script when the patient was uncomfortable was ridiculous.

"Did I stutter?" I asked, my contempt coming out. Tracey definitely 'ohh'ed behind me.

Hands balled at his side tight, hard enough to make his knuckles white. His face turned a deep red before he sputtered, "How dare you tell me how to practice medicine? Do you know who I am?"

I pushed my chair back from the desk and crossed my legs casually. "I'm giving you the information."

"I will not have a simple nurse tell me what to do." His face twisted in disgust. Better docs than him have called me worse. The words didn't faze me. "You will not tell me, a physician, what to do or what to prescribe a patient. I will perform an exam, provide a diagnosis, then tell *you* what to do." He spit out the last words.

In confrontation, my history was to either cry or laugh. Laughter bubbled up in my throat as I pushed my chair back. "Okay, well... let me get the stirrups for you."

"What?" Confusion creased his face. "What?"

"The stirrups. You want to exam the patient yourself because I'm nothing but a nurse with over twenty years of experience and can't tell you what a yeast infection looks like. Besides, the admission urine sample confirms it." I shrugged just as laughter erupted from me. "Tracey, we still got some stirrups in the supply closet?"

Tracey wouldn't turn around and was curled up in her station, shaking with laughter. "Na, Lexi, we sent those down to the emergency room a while ago."

I wiped tears from my eyes. There was no controlling it. "Well, Doctor Nakamura. Looks like either you'll have to wait for us to go get them or you can take the word of a simple nurse and the lab results for what it is."

"You are the most disrespectful woman I've ever dealt with."

"Oh, I find that hard to believe." I sat down and pulled my chair to the desk, back straight. My fingers played along the laminate edge of the desk, found a seam, and rubbed it back and forth.

His lips pursed. "Fine, I'll sign off on the orders this time." He shook a finger in my face. "But next time you call me when you even think a patient has something going on. All of you." He waggled his finger around the unit at us. "I'll make the diagnosis here. I'm the clinician," he huffed and stormed away.

"And you're the asshole, too," Tracey said, once he disappeared. A smile broke out on my face, and I turned to respond to her when Nakamura flew around the corner again.

"You're Lexi Burns, aren't you?"

I barely nodded, laughter dead. "Guilty."

"You're the one that keeps questioning my death certificate." His finger appeared in my face again. "I should have known."

I debated about biting off the offending digit but thought better of it. Zelda would approve but wouldn't loan me money when I lost my job, then my license to practice for assault and battery.

"I've caused you problems? What about the pain you've caused by declaring a death an accident when you must realize it's a murder?" Anger rose in my cheeks. "Or are you as incompetent in telling the difference between a murder and an accident as you are reading a message and signing a simple order?"

Tracey got up from her chair and stood next to me. She was no longer laughing.

Nakamura straightened his jacket, and a smug smile spread across his face. "I know, for a fact, you've been told to stay away from the case. Clearly, you've taken your..." his smile widened, "frustrations out on another matter. This will be discussed with the nursing manager."

"That's fine, Dr. Nakamura. Just remember, I asked for a simple order, and you came down here and started drama, disrupting my unit." I held up my hands. "I'm just doing my job." I left the words "unlike yourself," hanging silently in the air between us.

Nakamura stalked off. Tracey waited a moment before stepping out of the unit and glancing down the hall. "Okay, he's gone." She turned to me. "What crawled up his ass?"

I dropped my head into my shaking hands. "You remember that code a few days ago?"

"The girl that came in all torn up by an animal or something." She shook her head. "Sure. Nobody but a sadist would forget the gossip about the wounds she sustained."

"Nakamura signed off on it as an accidental death. But too many things don't add up."

"Ah," Tracey dropped into her chair. "No wonder he has a hard on for you. Men don't enjoy having their decisions questioned, honey, especially not a doctor." She patted my back. "You care too much."

I sighed hard, waiting for my nerves and emotions to come to an equilibrium. "If it was me or someone I loved laying on a slab, torn up like that, I'd want someone to care. Someone to fight for me. For the truth."

The last words came out shaky and tear-choked. That was it. That was the reason why I did what I did every day. That's the reason I couldn't let Buffy's murder go.

Tracey squeezed my shoulder. "I understand, Lexi. Have you talked to someone about this?"

"No, I don't need to see anyone. I need the truth. If it was me I was laying in the morgue—or someone I loved—I'd was, I'd want somebody one to give me the same respect." My voice dissolved into hysterics, and I excused myself to the bathroom.

In the mirror, my face was blotchy and eyes red. The tears flowed. Seeing how little regard Nakamura had for anyone broke my heart.

Chapter Eighteen

I splashed cold water on my face and focused on breathing. Once my hands stopped shaking, I texted Zelda.

—Hey, how are you feeling today?—

—Jail isn't that different from high school when you're talking to administration about putting in my retirement papers.—

I laughed out loud. Both of us had twenty years in. I wasn't sure about getting retirement benefits, but I had a good amount of savings set by. But what would we do with the rest of our lives?

—I hear you. I'm seriously looking into travel nursing.—

—No idea what I'll do, but after recent days I'm done. Would you believe Nate brought me flowers? Ugh.—

She liked my earlier comment and the "…" appeared on the screen, then added,

—I feel like I already know the answer, but do you want to stop trying to find Buffy's killer?—

—Not a bit. I just had a run in with Nakamura. Total douche.—

—Haven't had the pleasure. Private school… Call me after work and fill me in.—

I gave her text a thumbs up, dried my face and plodded back to the unit. I did a quick check of my patients before I clocked out. The patient in room ten-A was asleep and showed stable vital signs. He should go home tomorrow. The post-op ruptured appendix in 14-B wasn't doing great, still lots of pain and fever three days after surgery. I left a message for the doctor to stop by. Nakamura still hadn't signed off on the medication order for the patient's yeast infection so I asked the nurse from the oncoming shift to follow up before as I grabbed my tote and left.

At home, I started a dinner of grilled chicken and sauteed Brussel sprouts with balsamic vinegar and mustard. As the pan sizzled, I popped open a bottle of wine, filled it near almost to the rim, and drank deeply. My shoulders and neck were rock hard. I swiveled my head in a stiff circle, then side to side, then shrugged a couple times in an attempt to loosen the muscles with no luck. I was too old for long shifts and confrontations with assholes. Perhaps it was time to follow Zelda's lead and file my termination paperwork.

I called Zelda and it went straight to voice mail. She might be in an after-school class or a faculty meeting. She'd eventually see the missed call notification and get back with me when she was free.

Once my dinner was ready, I carried the plate and my wineglass to the living room and settled on the couch. After turning on the television, I channel surfed for a while but sparked my attention. The food smelled delicious, but I pushed it around the plate, taking a few bites but not tasting it.

I got up and poured myself another glass of wine and left the plate on the kitchen counter. My phone dinged with an alarm notification. Someone was at the door seconds before the door shivered with a bang. I sat the glass down on the coffee table before the door shook again.

"Lex! Lex! Open up!" Zelda yelled, and the door shook again.

I threw open the door and Zelda bolted past me, slamming the door behind her.

"What the hell, Zel?" I exclaimed. She was breathing heavy, hair frizzy, and eyes wide.

"Give me a minute," she huffed and dropped on the couch before grabbing the wine glass and downing it. "Do you have any more of this?" She held the glass out to me.

I took the glass and refilled it before filling one for myself. Back in the living room, she took the glass from me with thanks. "Did you run here from somewhere? Zel, what's going on?" I took a seat next to her.

Zelda drained the glass and burped. "No, my car is outside but...Girl... you will not believe what happened." Her face was etched in fear. "Celeste Stephens is missing."

I almost slid off the couch. "What?"

Zelda rolled the wineglass stem between her hands. "After the police said Dylan came up missing, I wondered if someone might be taking out witnesses. I checked on Neveah; she's fine but I put an extra strong sigil around the entire house, then buried a jar near the stoop."

"Good for you to think of that, Zelda," I told her. "I'm proud of you."

She took a deep breath, let it out on a hiss. "Yeah, well, wait till I tell you the rest." After chugging on the wine, she took another deep breath. Clearly, she was upset and looked close to tears. "From Niveah's place I drove to Celeste's, took a bag of herbs and some protective stones."

"Okay, and?" I asked.

She glanced at me, tears flooding her eyes. "I found the door open and her purse and wallet were sitting on the kitchen counter. Her cane was by the front door."

My stomach dropped. Celeste would not have left her home without those things. With her bad hip, she didn't go anywhere without the cane. And, as we used to say in nursing school, she was one of those women who considered her purse with the same importance as her uterus. She never left home without it.

"Did you call the police?" There was no way Zelda would get out of this if the police found out she'd been at Celeste's house."

She shook her head. "Even if I called anonymously, I don't trust those sneaky bastards to not put it on me."

"But what if she's hurt? We have to tell someone."

"That's why I came straight here. There's something else, Lex." Her breath came in hitches. Her hand shook as she pulled a cell phone out of her pocket and held it towards me. "I found this on the porch."

I took the cell phone, and the screen lit up. The home screen had a photo of Dylan and a young blonde girl. I recognized the photo from his social media, the same one I saw when I researched him. My guts fell to my feet. "Shit."

Zelda dropped against the sofa cushions. "Exactly."

"You shouldn't have taken this. It's evidence."

She squeezed her eyes shut and rubbed her forehead. "I don't know what I was thinking. It puts Dylan at Celeste's house and they're both missing."

I held the phone in my hand, unable to let go. It had

my fingerprints on it as were Zelda's. Even if we wiped it clean, the police could trace it to within a few miles of my house, if not my exact house. It didn't matter what we did, we were deeper in this than we needed to be.

"Lex, what do we do?" Fear laced her words.

I took in Zelda's shaking hands and scrunched face. Little scared her or put fear in her. Squirrels and her Grandma Francis, but that's about it. I shook my head. "Let me think." I put the phone on the coffee table and wiped my sweaty palms down the legs of my pants. "We have to call someone about Celeste. She's on meds she has to take or she's going to end up in the ER. Or worse." My brain raced. "That's it. We'll call in an anonymous and request a wellness check on an elderly person."

Zelda's brow furrowed at my suggestion, and she let out a groan.

"If it does get traced back to me, I'm a nurse and have seen her at the hospital. I can say I was worried about her."

Zelda shook her head. "That won't work."

"Why not? That's what a well person check is, isn't it?"

"But if you're concerned, why don't you go check on her? People who are familiar with you, know that you would go check on her yourself, Lex. Then someone—like Scott or one of his coven—might ask what made you concerned? You're not in a clinic."

I raised both hands. "Okay—I, uh—happened to see her at the grocery store, and she looked off. I would have stopped by her place to check on her, but I'd promised Scott not to get involved anymore."

"Not a bad theory for an anonymous call that's not anonymous," Zelda said as I picked up my cell phone and dialed the non-emergency police number. The operator answered promptly, and I gave them the info. My voice was calm and even, like I was giving a report to a fellow nurse. As I spoke into the cell, Zelda walked into the kitchen to refill her wine glass."

The police operator assured me an officer would do a wellness check as soon as possible, we disconnected. Zelda had found the remains of my dinner. She lifted the fork to her mouth and her eyebrow raised. "This isn't bad." She brought the plate and glass into the living room.

"Glad you're enjoying it. The police will go by." I sat back down on the sofa, tucking my legs under me. "Now, what to do with that?" I pointed to Dylan's phone.

Zelda stared at it a long time. "Ugh, right? What if we wipe it down and throw it in the trash somewhere? Like at the gas station behind Celeste's house?"

The gas station behind her house had the best donuts in town. They had a small kitchen and made them all day so you could go in almost any time of day for a fresh donut. The proximity to Celeste's house didn't hurt, either. "Let's go now, throw it in and get a donut for cover."

Zelda jumped off the couch, returned her plate to the kitchen. "Let's go. I could use a diet soda."

I followed her to the door. "I'm driving."

At the gas station, I grabbed some trash from the back seat and threw it and the phone in the can out front. Not before wiping it down with hand sanitizer and scrubbing it well. We got a dozen donuts and two big sodas before heading back to my house.

On the drive home, Zelda talked about starting the retirement process and how freeing it was. The word of her time at the police station hadn't gotten out yet, but when it did, the process would speed up. I recounted my interaction with Nakamura at the hospital earlier. By the time we got back to my house, we were short several donuts and most of the sodas.

"Why don't you run for county Coroner?" Zelda asked, her mouth filled with sprinkles and glaze.

I laughed. "What?" I opened the front door, juggling the drink and donuts, and groped for the light switch.

"Seriously, you understand medical stuff, and you're the most honest person I've ever met. You would be great at it." Zelda bumped into me when I came to a stop.

In the dark shadows of the kitchen stood a huge, hairy beast, its back to us. Hair covered the body. A snuffling noise came from its mouth.

The monster turned toward us. Donuts and drinks splashed to the floor. Though the gloom hid its face, malice filled the space between us.

Chapter Nineteen

The beast launched itself in our direction. Zelda and I shoved each other, scrambled for the front door, then practically fell down the front steps, screaming and yelling the whole way.

She ran off to the left. I raced to follow her but when a neighbor's front porch light came on, I veered across the street toward it. Zelda followed.

Their front door opened, and Chester Dennis stood with his hands on his hips. "Now what's this all about?"

I pushed past him into the living room. Zelda dragged him inside then slammed the door closed. His wife, Shirley, sat at the dining table with her dinner in front of her.

We both started talking and waving our arms at the same time. Zelda had to stop to take a breath, but I kept going. "We came home from getting donuts at the Quick Stop and there was someone in my kitchen."

Chester's eyebrows shot up. "Someone broke in? To your house?" He turned to look through the through the peephole of the front door.

"It wasn't someone," Zelda gasped. "It was a monster."

"A monster?" Shirley asked from the dining room. She pushed herself up from the chair to join us in the formal living room. "Girls, there aren't such a thing as monsters."

"Let me call the police and get them over here." Chester removed the phone clipped on his hip. "Shirley, let's get these girls some water. You all have a seat." He motioned for us to sit on the plastic covered couch. We took seats slowly as the couch squeaked with our weight.

Shirley brought us glasses of ice water and we thanked her before gulping it down. Chester finished the call and took a seat in one of the two overstuffed leather recliners facing the big screen television. "Police are on their way. Are you two girls doing okay? Ya'll looked like you've seen ghosts."

I shook my head. "There was someone– something—in the kitchen. I have an alarm system." Fueled with adrenalin, my brain was racing.

"I don't remember you setting it when we left," Zelda said, still out of breath.

Shit. What are the chances of the one time I didn't use the alarm something would happen?

Shirley stood at the door and turned the knob. "I don't hear nothing. Would we hear the alarm if it was going off?"

"It's loud. I just put it in earlier in the week."

Chester raised one hand, palm out. "Don't open that door, Shirl. Not until the police get here." He turned to us. "Just in case. We don't want whatever's out there to be coming in here. They might take my porkchop." He and Shirley laughed.

It took Zelda a minute, but then she laughed too loud. All I managed was a smile. Shirley's pork chops and greens were legendary, but the combination of sugar and soda wasn't sitting well in my stomach.

She took a seat in the other recliner and pushed a button to automatically raise her legs.

"Did it yourself, uh? Been thinking about getting one of those doorbell cameras." Chester leaned back to pull back the curtain and look and looked out the window. "Nobody here yet."

"You should get back to dinner," Zelda suggested. "We can just sit here and wait."

Chester waved his hand. "Nah, that's not a problem. Those pork chops are just as good reheated as when they come out of the skillet."

"Sure are. They're also as good the next day, with some bar-be-que sauce,." Shirley added.

My stomach grumbled, and I put a hand over my stomach. "Sorry."

Shirley hit the switch to lower the leg rest on the recliner. "Nonsense. Here we're talking about food, and I bet ya'll haven't eaten. Come into the dining room and get a plate." She motioned for us to follow. I opened my mouth to protest, but Zelda was up and on Shirley's heels. I shook my head and followed.

Zelda already had a plate and was filling it with greens, a porkchop, and cornbread. Shirley handed me a plate, and I filled it with much of the same. While we ate, Shirley kept a running commentary going while about what makes the best greens and fried pork chops. I half listened, regretting not being able to give her my full attention. Shirley's pork chops were blue ribbon winning.

A silence settled through the house, only broken by our silverware clicking on the plates. "Police aren't here yet?" Shirley asked.

Chester grunted from the living room. "Nope, don't know what's taking them so long. These girls might have been murdered and the culprit halfway across the state by now."

Shirley grimaced. "Chester, don't talk like that. The girls are right here. They don't need any more things to be afraid of."

I ducked my head and shoved a forkful of greens in my mouth. The fact they both kept calling us girls made me chuckle. Shirley and Chester had kids our age, but it had been a long time since anyone thought of Zelda and me as kids.

Blue and red flashing lights appeared through the curtains. Chester stood. "Well, looks like they made it." He motioned to us. "Finish up what you're eating and let's head over."

We did as we were told and followed him across the street. The police car sat out front had turned its lights off and the officer was getting out of the car.

"Hey, young man," Chester waved at the officer as we approached.

The officer returned the wave. "What's going on tonight, sir?" he asked, tone guarded.

"I'm the one that called you out. Looks like these two girls came home and found someone in the kitchen." Chester gestured to me. "I heard them scream and turned on the porch light. They came over and we've been waiting since."

The accusation that the officer had taken his time to get there hung in the air.

"Sorry about that, folks. There's only two of us on duty tonight and we had a wellness check to do."

Zelda and I exchanged a side eye look. If the officer knew it was us who requested the that called the well check, he didn't show it.

"Ladies, let me go look inside and you all wait out

here." We all nodded, and the officer approached the front steps. The door stood opened to the darkness beyond. I was sure I'd left a light on when we left. Even a couple of lights.

I shook my head. We watched the officer's flashlight beam travel through the windows. He finally came out and clipped his flashlight onto his belt. "This is ya'll's house?" he asked Zelda and me.

"It's mine," I said. "We ran out for donuts and came back to find something in the kitchen."

He nodded. "I saw the food m smashed up in the foyer. Well, there was someone in there for sure. Did you get a look at them before ya'll ran out?"

Zelda exhaled sharply next to me. I reached for her hand and grasped it tightly. "No," I said, "it was dark." I wanted to add you wouldn't believe me if I told you, anyway.

"There are muddy footprints in the kitchen and out the back. Looks like that's how they came in."

"The back door? Was it unlocked?" I shook my head. That door was rarely used, and I always kept it locked and bolted.

"You're going to need to call a handy man or someone to fix the door. Looks like they used a crowbar to bust it open," the officer said.

"No need for that. Let me grab my tools." Chester was already jogging across the street before I protested.

"I can't believe someone broke in. I just installed an alarm."

"Must have forgotten to turn it on." The officer shook his head. "I do that, too. I ask myself all the time why I have an alarm if I don't use it. Let's go inside and see if anything is missing." He held out his arm for us to lead.

I held fast to Zelda's hand and walked up the front steps. The officer had turned on the kitchen and living room lights. It was my house, but it wasn't. The coffee table was overturned, a leg broken. Someone had ripped the couch cushions open, and stuffing strewed everywhere. Kitchen barstools laid on the ground.

I dropped Zelda's hand and walked through the kitchen. They had emptied the fridge and cabinets then tossed the contents everywhere.

"Is the entire house like this?" I asked, my voice a whisper. I did not know how I could clean all of this up or what I'd need to replace.

The officer was at my shoulder. "Nope, just downstairs. Looks like they were looking for something. You probably interrupted them before they got upstairs. Might still be able to sleep up there tonight." His voice was kind, but I couldn't imagine spending the night here.

"She's spending the night with me," Zelda said before she disappeared upstairs to the bedroom. "I'm packing a bag for her."

"Is anything missing that you know of?" the officer asked.

Tears welled in my eyes. The kitchen cannister my grandma made for me in her ceramics class lay shattered on the tiled floor. I exhaled hard and rested my hands on my hips.

"Ma'am," the officer said. "I'm sorry you have to go through this. This was probably just a druggie looking for something to sell for their next score. I'll write up the report and send you a copy to sign. If you find anything missing, let me know. Can I get your email?"

I gave him my personal email, and he thanked me

and handed me a business card before leaving. He passed Chester and Shirley on the way out. Chester let out a low whistle when he took a look inside the house.

"Lord, have mercy," Shirley exclaimed behind him. "Someone sure was looking for something.

"What?" I asked, pulled from my thoughts. My hand fidgeted with the hem of my top, finding the seam and tracing the stitching.

Shirley blinked and shook her head. "Look around. Somebody wanted something."

I glanced at the carnage, this time with fresh eyes. As Shirley said looked like someone had been searching for something. But what? All the jewelry I owned I wore every day. I didn't keep more than a hundred dollars in the house anymore. What would I have that someone would want?

"Lord, Shirley, now you're really going to scare the girl." Chester had moved to the back door and sat his toolbox on the ground. He opened and closed the door, examining the damage. "She won't want to live here anymore, then we'll end up with a crap neighbor."

Zelda came down the stairs with my overnight bag over her shoulder. "Ready to go?"

"I… I'm going to stay here." My voice shook.

A chorus of no's rang around the room. "Not a chance, sweetheart," Zelda said, already heading for the door.

"I wouldn't recommend it," Chester offered. "I'll get the door fixed tonight, but it's going to be some banging and will keep you up. Best you go with your girlfriend and come back tomorrow."

"Uh huh, get some rest tonight." Shirley nodded, wrapping an arm around my shoulder, and pulling me towards the door.

I threw my hands up in defeat. "Fine."

"Go on, Lexi. We'll stay here and lock up. Do you have a code for the alarm?" Chester asked.

I pulled out my phone and gave him a temporary code from the app.

"Okay, now go. We'll take care of stuff here." He and Shirley nodded and walked me to the door.

Once we got out of the house, Zelda turned around. "You okay?"

"Do we take your car or mine? Should I drive?" I asked her, unsure. I was the confident one, the one that took control of things, that fixed things. Being helpless was a new feeling for me—and an uncomfortable one.

She took me by the arm and led me to the passenger side of her car. "I don't think driving right now is a good idea. You look like you're in shock."

She closed the door and walked around to her side. After putting the overnight bag in the back seat, she sat in the driver's seat and started the engine.

"Something was in my house, Zel." The tears flowed and the shock left my body weak as exhaustion set in.

She shook her head. "It was a someone, Lex. It was a *someone* in a costume. Why would anyone do that? I do not know." She shrugged. "But that's what it was."

I nodded and let the tears fall. We drove in silence to Zelda's house. She parked in the garage and waited until the door was fully closed before getting out of the car. Inside the house, she put me and my overnight bag on the bed before giving me a hug, turned on the nightstand light and closed the door.

I washed my face and changed into a nightgown

before pulling back the floral sheets and slipping between them. My eyes closed quicker than I thought possible. I thought I'd be awake for hours. Instead, I barely woke up the next morning.

The bright sun was fully in the room. Panic set in immediately. I had to be at the hospital at eight. I reached for my phone but didn't find it. And I couldn't remember when I had it last. Throwing the blankets off, I hurried out of the bedroom to Zelda's kitchen. She was sitting in her robe, drinking a cup of coffee at the table. The newspaper in her hands.

"What time is it? I'm late for work."

She dropped the paper and picked up my cell phone, waving it. "No, you're not. I called in for both of us last night before I went to bed. After all that excitement, I figured we both could use a day off."

I nodded and dropped into a chair across from her.

She stood and ambled to the kitchen. "Let me get you a cup of coffee and something to eat."

I groaned and dropped my head to my folded arms on the table as all of the events from last night hit be again. Zelda returned and set a cup of creamy mocha in front of me and a plate of some sort of bread. I sniffed it. Bananas.

"When do you have time to cook?" I asked as I shoved a bite into my mouth and washed it down with the rich coffee.

"I didn't. A grateful parent gave it to me for his kid getting a perfect score on his pre ACT test," Zelda winked. "He's a single dad with a baking hobby that will use any excuse to bring me something." She shrugged. "He's improving. I couldn't stomach his brownies." She made a gagging face, and I laughed.

Zelda always had a ton of admirers but didn't pay most of them any attention. Her carefree attitude and straight shooting manner attracted all sorts of men. It was something I'd envied when we were younger. Now, I appreciated it.

"It's pretty good." I took another bite.

She sipped her coffee. "He takes direction well."

"A replacement for Nate?" She hadn't mentioned him, and I wondered what was going on with them.

She grimaced and set the cup down. "Eh? Is it bad that I don't really want to deal with any of them? Like, is it bad to want to be the crazy cat lady?"

"As long as I'm allergic, it is." I smiled.

She shrugged, then tilted her head to the side. "True, I guess we can't move to Miami and spend time on the lanai if you're constantly sneezing and coughing." She made a face at me and drained her cup. "Nate's not a bad guy but... something isn't right..."

I nodded. "You keep saying that. Might it be our dislike of commitment and love of freedom that makes you want to have absolutely nothing to do with him?"

"Maybe it's me, but there's something not right." She popped another bit of bread into her mouth.

It was more than his love of silk shirts and combat boots that was odd with Nate. I didn't want to hurt Zelda's feelings or say anything negative about him, but he was the type of person I wasn't comfortable with, and I didn't know why.

"Since we aren't going to work today, how about we do three things?" Zelda held up her hand. "First, let's go clean your place up." I nodded. "Second, then we'll get lunch at the Mexican place that puts the little cornmeal patties on all the plates." She held up two fingers, and I nodded. Those were yummy little cakes. "And third, we're planning a trip to somewhere warm with strong drinks." I opened my mouth to say no, but her expression made me shut my mouth. "Nope, we haven't been on a vacation in years. Years! Life is too short."

I couldn't argue with her. Last I checked, I had over three weeks of vacation saved and almost a month of PTO—personal time off. "I'm down for two of the three. We'll see on the trip."

"Hmph, either you plan it with me, or I do it myself and charge your card," Zelda said over her shoulder as she took our dishes to the kitchen. "Go get dressed."

I followed instructions and dressed in the leggings and T-shirt she'd packed the night before.

When we got to my house, Zelda parked in the driveway. My car was nowhere to be seen. Had someone come back to steal it? I pulled up the alarm app and saw Chester didn't use the code until five in the morning.

"Didn't you leave your car in the driveway when we left last night?"

"Yes, and Chester didn't use the alarm until five in the morning." I got out of the car and Zelda followed. "Watch, he forgot to set the alarm and came back when he woke up this morning. Probably giving someone time to steal the car."

This is what I got for trusting someone and not doing it myself.

I used the app to turn off the alarm and unlocked the door. The smell of lavender cleaner and soap hit me. The house was spotless and perfect. The only thing missing was the couch cushions. Other than that, there was no way to know anything happened last night.

"Wow," Zelda said behind me. "What happened?"

"No idea. Perhaps cleaning fairies?" I chuckled.

Leave it to me to hunt werewolves and end up with house fairies. I dropped my tote bag on the kitchen island and inspected the kitchen. What had been a disaster zone last night was spotless now. Not a crumb in sight. On the counter sat by grandma's cannister, glued back together. I held it up and hugged it close.

Chapter Twenty

"Okay, well, I don't know how this happened, but I say we can knock one thing off our list. Want to grab lunch?" Zelda asked brightly.

"Hold on, I'd rather find out how this got done." I examined the back door. It was fully repaired and would pass for brand new. "It couldn't have been Chester and Shirley?"

"Did I hear my name?" Chester came in the front door, with Shirley trailing behind him. Both of their arms filled with couch cushions. They settled them on the couch, smoothing them down. "How you girls doing this morning?"

"Chester, did ya'll do all this?"

He waved the question away. "Don't even think about it."

"You had to be up all night, worked all night," I insisted.

Shirley nodded. "We sure did, but don't worry. We don't sleep much anymore anyway. It was good to get up and do stuff." She wrapped an arm around Chester's waist and smiled up at him. "Good to be helpful again."

"That's right. Since we retired, we're useless." He wrapped an arm around her shoulders and laughed. "No good to no one." They both smiled and laughed at their joke. "Seriously though, it's what neighbors do."

I hugged them both. I realized exactly how lucky I

was to have them. Releasing them, I examined the cushions. "Did you sew these, Shirley?"

She nodded. "Sure did. Didn't take any time at all on the sewing machine. The rips were smooth, like done with a sharp knife. Easy peasy." She laughed again. "It was good to get the machine out. Hadn't used it in a bit."

"Well, I can't thank you enough. Can I take you to lunch or something?" I asked, dumbfounded. They had done nice things all up and down the neighborhood, but this seemed above and beyond.

Chester waved it off again. "Nah, we're going to have some lunch and then a nap. Don't worry, it's not because we stayed up doing this." He waved his arm around. "We take a nap every afternoon now that we're retired. By the way, I put your car in the garage. So no one got any ideas."

Shirley laughed again. "Getting caught up before we die." Tears appeared at the corner of her eyes from her joke.

I said thank you again, and we exchanged goodbyes and promised to get together soon. Cooking them a nice dinner was the least I could do for this wonderful couple.

After they left, Zelda walked around the house checking out their handiwork. "This is fantastic work. They should open a business."

"What? Like a 'your house got broken into and we come to the rescue' business?"

Zelda frowned. "No, but like a cleaning and handyman service. Nothing too crazy. Like what they did here."

"But that would cut into their nap time."

Zelda joined me sitting on the couch. "God forbid. Seriously, Lex. We need to change careers or do something. Definitely the trip, though."

I nodded. "I can't argue with you. I'm guessing you have some ideas of where to go?"

Zelda's face drew a blank. That meant she had ideas and probably dates already selected. "Well, I was considering Hawaii?"

I had never been to Hawaii, and it seemed like a dream place. Someplace rich people went, not me. I pushed that idea out of my mind. Years of hard work had paid off, and my savings account was comfortable.

"That's not a bad idea. You have an itinerary?" I asked, knowing full well she did.

"Yeah, it's a rough draft, of course. More of ideas for you, us, to pick from. And of course, you can add whatever you want." She shrugged. "Totally open to suggestions. I'll email it to you later. Let's grab some lunch."

"I can't argue with that." We stood and headed to the front door when my phone pinged with a notification from Scott.

—*Hey, just saw the report from last night. Are you guys okay? Is there a lot of damage?*—

I huffed and texted back, remembering he always listened to the police radio and had to know what happened when it happened last night, but didn't bother responding to the scene.

—*I'm good. Nothing I can't handle. Thanks.*—

I added, then erased several emojis before sending the text.

"Scott?" Zelda asked, an eyebrow raised.

I nodded. "He asked if everything was okay."

Zelda made a disapproving sound. "He could come over to arrest you but not to check on you after a break in—with clear and convincing evidence?" She nodded to herself. "Okay, makes total sense for that dipshit. Want to ask him what's going on with Celeste?"

I dropped the phone on the couch. "Not really. He'll start telling me to stay out of it again."

Zelda suggested we go to lunch again and we headed to a Mexican place for a bite.

The server was our usual and knew to bring a tub of guacamole and chips as soon as we sat down. Zelda's margarita and my beer soon followed.

"Did you notice what Shirley said about the cushions?" I asked as I popped the lime down the neck and took a swig.

"That the cuts were clean?" Zelda sighed after taking a sip of margarita and licking the salt from her lips. "Have to wonder if that was the same type of cuts that were on Buffy's neck."

I raised my eyebrow. "Clean, like a knife is what she said, right?" Zelda nodded. "Damn Nakamura for not measuring or photographing the wounds. If we had that we could compare them to what's on the couch."

Zelda's face scrunched up in thought. "His incompetence aside, I don't know that it would matter. Not to be morbid, but her neck and the cushions are different sizes. More room to work on one than the other." Color rose in Zelda's cheeks. "So to speak." And she took a gulp of alcohol. I didn't need to ask why. We were nonchalantly discussing knife wounds over guac. If she didn't blush, I'd worry about her.

The food was hot and great as always. It barely arrived when Nate walked by the table and stopped. "Babe, you didn't tell me you weren't going to be at school today. What's up?"

He leaned over to drop a kiss on Zelda's head. She didn't recoil fully, but there was a slight pull back and a downturn of her lips."I texted this morning about Lexi's house getting broken into," she said. "Why aren't you at school?"

"Well, I took a mental health day." He squeezed her shoulders and glanced at me. "Lexi, what happened?"

I explained the incident the night before and events up till this morning. Leaving out our continued investigation and downplaying the neighbor's involvement. I wasn't sure why I felt the need to do that, but it felt right.

Nate's brow furrowed. "Who would care about you? You're only a nurse."

If he wasn't Zelda's boyfriend, I would have disemboweled him right there at the table. Instead, I threw him a smirk and didn't bother keeping the sass out of my voice. "Like you're only a music teacher?"

Zelda's eyebrow rose.

He ignored my comment. "Anywhoo, I could come by and fix the door for you. I've got tools in the back of the truck. I've very good with my hands," he said like it was a done deal as he ran his hands over Zelda's back.

Zelda's glaze narrowed. "Since when are you handy? You won't even change a lightbulb in my kitchen last week."

I shook my head. "It's all good, thanks."

"Hmmm…. you two are nothing short of thrilling, aren't you?" He licked his lips suggestively, and I had to look down at my food to keep from gagging. "So, I guess you'll be going back to Lexi's house and finishing cleaning?"

"No. It's all finished. We have plans."

"The cameras caught nothing?" he asked, moving his hands to massage Zelda's neck. Right about then, her shoulders were up to her ears.

"What cameras?" I asked, too fast.

"Well, the cameras on the alarm system you installed," he said, like I was the proverbial ditzy female. "Did they catch anything?"

I rested my elbows on the table and leaned forward. Zelda's and my gazes locked over the fried enchiladas. She tilted her head to one side. "How did you know about the alarm, Nate? And the cameras?"

His hands stilled on Zelda's shoulders for a moment. "You told me. Don't you remember, babe?" He leaned over her for confirmation.

She shook her head. "Nope, don't think that ever came up in conversation." She made eye contact with him. "So, how did you know about it?

Nate glanced from Zelda to me, and back to Zelda. "Don't get your panties in a bunch, ladies. Zelda, you just don't remember telling me about it, but you certainly did." He bent down and kissed her. Open mouth, tongue visible, hand holding her jaw in place.

I looked away uncomfortably. How Zelda liked this guy I would never understand.

She successfully pulled away and raised a hand to his chest. He rested his hand on top of hers, obviously oblivious to the fact she was trying to push him away.

"We'll finish that later tonight, babe." He winked and strutted through the restaurant. More than a few stares followed him.

Zelda rubbed her back and groaned. "Good Lord, I almost threw my back out trying to get out of that kiss."

"When did he start that crap?" I asked. We'd gone

on a few double dates in the past and Nate had been his normal odd self, but nothing that creepy and uncomfortable.

She took a bite of rice and beans. "Recently. He thinks I'm spending too much time with you. It's like he lives in an alternate world." She rolled her eyes. "One where he's always right and I'm always wrong. Luckily, he's there to correct me."

"He's gaslighting you." Zelda's eyebrow raised. "That's exactly what he's doing. Not okay." I didn't want to come right out and say he's abusive and that she should dump him, but it was implied.

She took another bite of enchilada and pushed the plate away. "He was always kooky and that was part of his charm, but now he's absolutely weird. He complains about you all the time, that I spend too much time with you. The other day I was at the grocery store, and he showed up. He lives across town. Why was he at that particular grocery store? I mean it's nothing special."

My plate no longer held my interest. The food was heavy and greasy in my stomach.

Since there are only two grocery stores in town, I asked, "Do you think he's following you?"

She shrugged. "Why would he?" She sat silent for a moment, and I gave her time to come to a conclusion. "But yeah, maybe. And he knows stuff that I swear I haven't told him, Lex. Not just your alarm system, but the other day he asked how the cakes were at the bakery and if I liked my shower gel." She shivered. "I just bought it that same day. How could he know? I'm not that interesting."

I chose my words carefully. "Doesn't matter how interesting you are or aren't. It is him and whatever is going on in his head. What his reasoning is."

"So it's time to cut him loose. For all his faults, he's not a bad guy, you know. Just…too much in another world. Or plane of existence." Zelda made a face and wave for the server. "Let's get out of here." We paid the server and headed out to the car.

That other plane of existence was exactly what attracted Zelda to Nate in the first place. My shoulders inched down from my ears knowing she would soon break up with him.

Before we headed home, we did some shopping for a few new things to replace decorative items Shirley couldn't glue back together. Zelda found a cute vase for her guest bedroom.

While shopping, we discussed our next major life steps. Options considered included opening a bed and breakfast or becoming private detectives, but neither of us had any idea how to do those things. Unfortunately, not a lot of things mixed our vocational skills well. But I'd bet money if Zelda put her mind to it, she'd find something for us to do.

She dropped me and my bags off at my house. I waved as I turned off the alarm. In the foyer, I dropped the bags and headed to the bathroom. I shouldn't have had three lemonades at lunch, but they were so tasty. I gave my hands a quick rinse and opened the door. The phone dinged a notification from my tote by the door.

I sighed and remembered I should return Kavitha's text about meeting up tomorrow when a steel arm reached around me, and a blinding pain shot through my side. I had just enough time to register the animalistic hairy arm wrapped around my throat, cutting off my air before I passed out.

Chapter Twenty-One

Pain burned as agony coursed through my body. Something bit at my flesh and forced my limbs against my side. Wincing, I squinted to take in the space around me. A small, barred window at the top of the wall gave the area its only illumination. Darkness and shadows surrounded me. I pulled at my wrists again. Thick chains held me with enough space to almost stretch.

"What in the f--?" I shifted my weight and the plastic crinkled on a baby mattress covered with a furry-fleece blanket one could buy at any home store. Whomever put me here had something in mind that required keeping the plastic covering on the mattress.

Whatever they had in mind, I would not sit here and accept what they had planned. Even chained. I sniffed the air and caught scents of natural gas, damp, and laundry soap. The normally comforting scent of the laundry froze my heart. Not unusual, lots of houses in town were built in the fifties with similar layouts. The houses in Scott's neighborhood were like this. I was in someone's basement.

My mind spun, and I steadied my breathing to relax and focus. This wasn't a joke or kids playing around. It wouldn't do any good for me to freak out. I would only survive this by focusing on the details and nailing the perpetrators when I got out. I closed my eyes and leaned against the cool cement wall, willing myself to relax and focus. This wouldn't get me.

Heavy footfalls and the creak of wood carried to me. The gait was slow and cumbersome. Someone was coming down the stairs. They were carrying something awkward or might be injured. When it grunted, and I jumped, straining the bonds when the heavy fell to the floor on the opposite side of the only exit.

Suddenly, blinding light filled the doorway. I squinted at the figure filling the space. A low growl erupted into a growl, deep and earthy. The vibration bounced off the walls. I hunched to make myself as small as possible as a cry escaped me. The thing's chest heaved in the shadows. It crept towards me slowly bent over. The crouch of an attacking animal. I pulled further away, the metal restraints cutting my flesh.

It placed a grocery sack on the floor and grunted, then shoved the sack towards me with another grunt. I shook my head. This is it. I had to focus, take in all the details. Every inch, every color had to be recorded.

This close, I could see the monster was in costume. Synthetic, dark, wiry hair that was supposed to be a werewolf or a big-foot costume the outside. That's why Celeste hadn't seen its *dingly dangle*. Wisps of hair hung over its face. The mouth was a dark hole. I stifled a laugh at the insanity of the situation. Neveah had been right all along. It was a werewolf.

It squatted low and growled. Suddenly, the thing was on me. Something rough like sandpaper and sharp-edged dug into my skin. Whether hands or claws, I didn't know. The skin on my wrists ripped as I tried to lift my arms to defend myself, but the manacles hampered my defensive efforts. I felt muscles pulling ed and tearing ore all over my body. I tried to kick, but the thin fabric of my leggings shredded. The thing was exceptionally strong and heavy. When I screamed, the thing's face came even with mine, its hair brushing my face. The eyes were dark holes where no brightness lived. This close, I felt the rumbling growl in its chest and the familiar scent gagged me.

"Shhh…" My blood froze at the soft sound.

Then it laughed. A loud, wholly human laugh that dinged a bell of recognition in my head. Fear kept the thought from forming. Another hand raised and tore my clothes. Pain seared from the lacerations on my skin.

My breath came in gasps, and I squeezed my eyes shut, willing my intellect to remember every detail. It grunted again, and I forced myself to look at it. The thing pushed the bag to me and grunted again. I opened it and looked inside. There were bottles of water, sandwiches, chips, and various candy bars. Gas station food.

"Thanks." I was unsure of what do to. What to say. This situation went beyond my worst nightmares.

It grunted again and stood, stretching to its full height. This close, the person appeared impossibly big. Wide and tall. It left the chamber with a loping gait, almost skipping. The door closed and the lock slammed into place.

I leaned my head back and tried to assess my injuries. There were too many to count. Even if I could get out of the irons, I was behind a locked door and weak, mentally and physically. Squeezing my eyes shut, I took an inventory of what I learned, then cursing because it wasn't much more than what I knew before. Neveah and Celeste had been right all along. Since there was no point in focusing on the creature, thing. I had to focus on keeping my strength up and getting the details of this place.

I inhaled deeply and moved to poked at the contents, again, unsure whether I should ingest any of the contents. I inspected the seals on the food and bottles, holding it up in the dimness and feeling each item. It all looked safe. But was it? It might be poisoned. Either I took the chance on the poison or died of dehydration and starvation. Strength is what would get me through this. I unwrapped a candy bar. This situation was insane but giving into that would not be helpful. It wouldn't get me out of here or find Buffy's killer. I had to focus on the facts and not attempt to make sense of the insanity.

I grabbed the bottled water, its sides slick with moisture, and chugged. The water was cold and refreshing. I poked through the bag again and found a book and a small pocket flashlight. *The Beast of Gevaudan.* A history book? Interesting choice. The cover worn and pages fell out as I opened it. Reading would take my mind off the pain, soreness, and the crusting blood. A form of normalcy. I would worry about my injuries once outside. Until then, I would read and clear my mind until the thing came back.

****

I read and ate. As I ate, I struggled over every detail of this place in my mind. At some point, my head was mush and I fell into a fitful sleep. When I woke fully, the sunlight from the small window at the top of the wall faded. How many days had passed? The space became warmer and smelled of damp and earth. I tried to move around but the bonds kept me in one place. I shifted my legs and the mattress plastic crinkled loudly. The scent of the iron agitated my nose. My limbs were slick with sweat and crusty with dried blood.

The steps sounded again, slow and lumbering. I willed my heartbeat to slow down. I tucked the flashlight in my lap. The entry to my prison opened, and the figure grunted as it struggled to pull through the doorway. It pushed the bulky item toward me. In the dim glow, I made out the outlines of a camp toilet with blankets.

I shined the flashlight on the monster. The person covered its face with a mangy arm with an agitated grunt, a wholly human sound.

"Why am I here?" I demanded.

It grunted in response and turned to leave.

"Please, why am I here? Who are you?" My voice on the verge of hysterics. I willed my breathing to slow with no success.

The figure grunted again and waved a dismissive hand in my direction before slamming the door and throwing the lock.

My breath caught in my throat. How many times had I seen that hand gesture from Scott? How many times had he done that towards service people, and I turned the other way, ignoring his rudeness?

The monster couldn't be Scott. He was a detective. He might have behaved like a douche recently, but he had committed his life to service. Hell, he didn't even like when I drove through a yellow light. No, it couldn't be him.

I shook my head viciously, pain shooting down my spine. "No, no, no."

From somewhere above, a sound reached me. My ears strained. First, I heard static, then a female voice relaying numbers and codes, then more static. A police radio! The same type Scott kept on twenty-four- seven at his house. How many times had that provided background noise in the middle of the night?

It all came together. Scott's laundry room was in the basement. They had built his house in the nineteen fifties and had small basement windows with bars. Just like this house.

My recently ex-boyfriend, dressed as a werewolf, had kidnapped me.

Chapter Twenty-Two

I lost count on time by the way light moved through the barred window. It might have been a few days, or weeks. The costumed monster came and went, leaving a bag of junk food and water, but not before the thing would attack me, opening old wounds and creating new ones. Each one showed varying stages of infection. I willed myself not to think about the growing warmth from the wounds or the chills that racked my body. Did I imagine the redness around the cuts and lacerations in the pale light? A dry chuckled escaped me. If this thing didn't kill me, the infection most likely would. My plan to remember every detail of this place and the person was quickly lost to basic survival.

Anger and determination disappeared and left behind fear and agony. I didn't want this thing to be Scott. We had broken up, but we'd had good times, too. Memories of us tubing down a river in the summer, the scent of sunscreen and the taste of wine coolers became more fresh. His strong grip as he reached for me strengthened in my head.

That I had loved and slept with a person who might do this to me worse than anything. The questions swirled inside my head. Why would he do this? What did he have to gain? Scott could be a dick, but he didn't have an evil bone in his body.

Evil resided in every cell of this creature, from

marrow to skin and everything in between.

No, this isn't about me. It's all about whatever foolishness this person had experienced in his past. I never subscribed to true crime programs or armchair psychology theories, but I understood enough that often, there was no responsible reason for someone's actions. Whether cutting you off in traffic or keeping you hostage in a basement. This was about the person.

Did Scott have secret demons even I didn't realize? He came to town in his twenties. Might something horrible happened in his formative years that scarred him and turned him into made this monster?

No, I would have seen a hint. Some internal alarm would have sounded. It did when I dated one guy in college. In fact, it was so loud I grasped for excuses not to go out with him after we'd gone to an after- party. I found out later he had been arrested and convicted of assault on a date a few months later. And Scott had been an Eagle Scout. Or he said he was. Had I seen the photos at his grandparent's house? I couldn't remember.

Even in my sleep, I dreamed of Scott. Waking up next to him, his smile warming my heart. The sun streamed in, highlighting the blond streaks in his auburn hair, the brown and few gray hairs in his chin. He would reach for me and pull me tight to his chest, right before a clawed hand appeared from the blankets and ripped my naked flesh. I woke up screaming.

But Scott was a cop. If anyone knew how to cover up a crime, it would be someone in law enforcement. This is a small town, too. With Nakamura as the coroner and the Chief of Police thinking more of retirement than crime, it would be even easier to cover one up.

How long had I spent talking a loud to myself?

Trying to convince myself it wasn't Scott? My throat dry and my voice hoarse. Hours at least. Then the sound of the police radio filtering down would assault my ears, or he would start the washer or dryer. Normal domestic activities for him. Who else might it be?

I had convinced myself it couldn't be Scott when the creature brought in another bag of food and water. Too weak to reach for the bag or try to make an escape, I simply laid there and stared at it while he put the bag next to me. The scent of animal, blood, and something else—fainter but present—reached my nose.

Scott's cologne.

The thing snickered as it closed the door. Tears spilled down my cheeks. I understood.

Without a doubt in my heart, the creature that killed Buffy, most likely kidnapped Celeste, and was torturing me, was Scott.

Chapter Twenty-Three

I gave up on staying coherent. It was all Scott. I had misjudged everything. Why try to remember anything of this? I drifted on the edge of sleep, dreaming of laughing on a beach with Zelda, waves crashing into me and the sun warming my skin when a blinding light woke me. My body burned in the sun. I raised my arms, but they fell weakly to my side. I didn't see the taser even when the burning electricity surged through me, and the world turned black.

I woke frigid and wet. An icy breeze caressed my skin and ruffled my hair. Goosebumps covered my flesh. I opened my eyes, and more confusion filled my head. Above me was filled with the stars, bright and clear above me. I was outside. A whimper escaped me.

I was outside!

I tried to move my arms and legs, but the joints locked, muscles taunt and rigid. I did not know how long it had been since I had stood up. While chained to the wall, I did leg exercises and tried to move to keep myself strong. It hadn't been enough and after a point, I gave up. I took a deep inhalation e of the fresh air as warm tears coursed down my cheeks.

I took a deep breath, held it, and on the exhale, pushed myself up to sitting. Pain was everywhere. Every muscle, tendon, nerve, pulsed. It took four breath cycles to get to my elbows. Another ten to get to my knees, exhausted. There would be no standing. I collapsed against the tree Scott had left me under, the bark rough under my exposed skin. My clothes were filthy, and I stank. Someone sobbed. I glanced around hopeful for someone to help me but saw no one. It took me a minute to realize the sound came from me.

Streetlights towered in the distance. From somewhere to my left, a dog barked. Dark woods to my right. Behind me a small park, tendrils of fog wrapped around the playground equipment, giving the scene a dreamy quality. Had I died, and this was a dream? I moved my knees and legs against the soft, damp grass and pain ripped through me. No. Even hell wouldn't have this much agony.

Focusing on the streetlight just ahead, I crawled slowly. With each movement of my legs, pieces of myself were left behind. I lost count of the times I collapsed against the cool, soft grass before finding strength to continue. When I reached the pole, I clung to the freezing metal for support. The icy coldness shot pain through my hot flesh, and I recoiled.

My hold loosened, and I fell back to the ground. The cool grass was welcoming. I would stay here and rest until I had the energy again to stand. It wouldn't be long. I was fine. Car headlights passed me but didn't stop. I opened my mouth to scream, but no sound came out.

The cool grass and soft, fresh breeze comforted me. I had given up hope of ever getting out of that basement. When sleep came, I welcomed it and slipped dreamlessly into it. I did not know how long I laid at the base of the pole when the flashing red and blue lights washed over me. The squeak of the radio sent fear blooming all over again. Scott was here. He would take me back to the basement. Pain would soon follow. I wanted to run. I pushed myself up to crawl away, only to fall face first into the grass.

A hand touched my shoulder, gentle at first and then hard, grabbing me and holding me. Another hand grasped the other shoulder. "Ma'am? Ma'am, it's okay," a soothing female voice said. "You're safe now."

Whimpering, I stopped fighting and melted into the hands. The voice kept murmuring soothing words I couldn't make out.

I tried to yell, but only a whisper came out. "Scott…"

"Don't talk right now, honey."

More hands on me and more voices. Men's voice. I struggled and a mewing sound like a hurt kitten escaped me.

"My God, what happened to her?" A man's voice.

"Don't worry about that, just assess and stabilize," a different woman said. I heard her tone in my voice more than once that said focus on saving the patient and only that. The scales were tipping fast.

Hands moved in and a blanket, rough and thick, was draped over me. They lifted me into the ambulance, and I felt the sting of an IV being started. I pushed away the rising sense of claustrophobia. I was safe. Voices faded. Darkness followed. I welcomed it.

****

The aroma of hospital disinfectant seared my nostrils. A sense of overall cleanliness embraced me. The beeping of machines comforted me. I tried to open my eyes but failed. I had to blinked hard, several times, to loosen the sleep crusts. The room was dark, lit by a small lamp by a recliner next to the bed. As fear started to rise,

161

the machine alarms rose in volume.

A hand took mine and squeezed hard. "Lex? Oh, Lexi." Zelda's voice broke.

"What…" I tried to talk, but my throat was raw and painful. Zelda sat by my bed in the dim room filled with flowers. A television in the far corner flashed, the sound low.

"No, no. Don't talk. The nurse will be in soon." She patted my hand. "I'll go get some fresh water and ice."

I closed my eyes and tried to take a deep breath. From my scalp to my toes, every muscle screamed. I turned my head, and the world spun behind my closed eyes. I groaned.

"Hey, pretty lady," Tracey stood by the bed and patted my hand, a smile on her face.

I returned her smile. It felt good to see another familiar face. "Hey," I croaked out.

"Don't talk just yet. You had an endo tube in for awhile so your throat is probably still raw." As is routine for my unit, she checked my vitals manually against those relayed by the monitors, then made some notes on the flipchart at the foot of the bed.

With Kavitha hot on her heels, Zelda walked in with a pitcher and cup of water. "She doing okay?" Concerned etched her features.

Tracey nodded. "Yep, she's good." She considered me for a moment and tilted her head to the side. "She's looked better, that's for sure."

I smiled at her joke. "You too." I tried to sound tough and funny, but it was awkward even to my ears.

"Already giving sass," Tracey said, laughing. "Good to see it." She squeezed my hand and tears came to the corner of her eyes. She let go of my hand to wipe them away. "I've got other patients since we're short staffed with people not showing up to work, laying around, eating bonbons." Sniffing, she left the room.

"You know she refuses to let any other nurse take care of you on her shifts? She's been working doubles to watch over you." Zelda put a straw in the water and held it to my lips. "The woman is a machine."

I sipped the water and almost wept at the coolness sliding down my throat.

"Good, right?" She sat the cup on the moveable table in front of me. She took a seat next to the bed. "I was so worried about you, Lex." Her voice broke and a small sob came out.

"We didn't think you were going to make it for a while." Kavitha reached for my shoulder and stroked. One hand trailed down to my wrist where she took my pulse. Medical professionals were never off duty.

I shook my head. "Takes more...than that...," I managed.

Zelda laughed. "Don't I know." And wiped her tears away.

"What...happened?" I asked, sounding more like myself.

"I'm not sure I should be the one to tell you all that." Zelda sighed hard and wrapped her arms around herself. "You were missing for almost two weeks." She shook her head. "The police found you laying on the curb outside Santa Fe Park."

My heart skipped a beat. That park was down the street from Scott's house.

She laughed awkwardly and reached for my hand. "Apparently someone called in a dead body sighting. Guess you weren't totally, thoroughly dead, huh?"

"Just mostly dead," I said, referencing our favorite movie as kids.

Her eyes glazed over, and a genuine smile stretched across her face. "If only Miracle Max was here. All we have are doctors."

"Hey, now!' Kavitha said, reproachfully.

We laughed. It would hurt for a while, but I could get used to it if I was among the living.

"So," Zelda squeezed my hand again. "The ambulance brought you in here and here you are."

"Injuries?" I asked.

"You have multiple abrasions, contusions and lacerations, several deep enough to require stitches. Most were seriously infected." Kavitha squeezed my shoulder and her face twisted, struggling to remain neutral. "Romping."

Huh. Kavitha saved *romping* for the really bad cases. She completed her report. "You're loaded up on antibiotics and IV fluids. Even after you started breathing on your own and we extubated you, we've administered sedatives to keep you relaxed. It was touch and go for a while. You've been with us in the hospital for five days."

"Jesus," I whispered. Five days…I was closer to the Pearly Gates than I knew.

"Yeah, I gave up on that dude a few years ago. I've been praying to Morrigan instead. Seems to turn out all right." Tears fell down Zelda's cheeks as she squeezed my hand. "I can't imagine life without you, Lexi."

Exhaustion took the words from me, and I squeezed her hand before I sunk into sleep.

****

When I woke next, Zelda was gone and the room

was deathly quiet. I found the remote device and pushed the button to elevate the head of the bed. For the first time, I got a good look at my arms. Even in the low light my arms were criss- crossed with cuts and stitches like a bad patchwork doll. Slowly, I reached for the cup of water and brought it to my lips. I tried to adjust my position, but everything hurt.

A shadow fell over the doorway. Scott. My heart raced and my blood froze. I screamed, and it came out strangled and pitiful.

His face contorted. He moved closer. I screamed louder, an inarticulate sound like a cornered animal. The water and tray crashed to the ground.

"Lexi, babe…" His hands reached for me, but instead of hands they morphed into claws.

Alarms on more than one machine blared as Tracey flew into the room. She pushed Scott aside and leaned over me. "Lexi, what is it? What's wrong?"

I couldn't take my eyes off him, nor could I stop screaming. Tracey grasped me by the shoulders, trying to calm me down. "Lexi, honey, please."

I huddled into her arms. "He did it," I gasped. "He hurt me."

With the little strength I had, I lifted my arm and pointed at Scott.

Then I passed out.

Chapter Twenty-Four

The next time I woke, the visitor's chair was pulled close to the bed, and Zelda's head rested on the mattress. She snored softly, occasionally sawing hardwood. Her hand gripped mine. I didn't want to wake her, but my fingers flexed by themselves. Her head shot up. Hair standing in all directions and eyes bleary.

"What? Lex, you okay?" Her voice thick.

Swallowing hurt less. "Okay." My head jerked to the doorway as I remembered Scott standing there earlier. It was empty, and I exhaled. "Not here."

Zelda's brow furrowed and relaxed. "Scott?" I nodded furiously. The pain was manageable now. "He left and I don't guess he'll be back. He sent flowers, though."

She pointed to a bouquet of wildflowers, my favorites, and patted my arm. "Lex, honey. Why did you get upset when he was here? Can you tell me?"

I motioned for a cup of water. Zelda filled the new glass and handed it to me. I took a drink, savoring its coolness before I started. "Scott, he kidnapped me." I didn't recognize the smallness and pain in my voice. "He hurt me."

She stood and wrapped her arms around me and held me tight against her. We stayed like that for a long time, Zelda crooning soothing sounds into my hair.

When we separated, tears streamed down her face,

leaving trails on her foundation and her eye makeup smeared. She grabbed a tissue and dabbed her face.

Sniffing, she handed me the cup of water again and I drained it. She dropped into the chair and exhaled. "Lexi, honey. I don't know how to tell you this." Her shoulders shrugged. "Scott wasn't the one who hurt you."

"No, no, he was…" I protested, but the words came out strangled.

She held up her hands to stop me. "Save your strength, honey. You were gone a while and then out of it here. A lot has happened." She closed her eyes and her lips moved silently in what I knew was a prayer. "We didn't want to tell you until later when you're stronger, better. But it looks like now is as good of a time as any."

I dropped back against the bed. I had no choice but to listen. I nodded and motioned for her to go on.

She ran the tissue across her face again. "The cops who made the wellness check on Celeste found her in the basement of the house. She'd been dead for a while. They think it happened not long after we left her the last time. She'd been strangled with her robe belt. Pretty shitty."

Zelda's face contorted in pain. "They found Dylan in an alley near the haunted house. The theory is he hid Celeste's body and was going to commit suicide, but he was jumped in the alley. Probably a vagrant or a druggie. No wallet or anything. They found him behind a dumpster. Things…animals…had gotten to him." A wry smile on her lips. "I guess he was in the wrong place at the wrong time. They found a note confessing to all the crimes in his pocket. Including kidnapping you and hiding you in an abandoned house's basement."

Ignoring the pain, I shook my head. "No. No. No. Someone was there. I heard footsteps. I heard sounds of laundry being done, smelled detergent and fabric softener. He was there all the time. I listened to the police radio."

Even to my ears, I sounded crazy. "You have to believe me."

Zelda patted my hand. "I know it seemed like it, but in the letter, he said he laced your food with LSD. God only knows what you experienced."

I raised my arms up for her, showing the deep cuts and stitches. "This is real. Someone was there. Someone did this." I dissolved into tears. "Please, Zel. Please, understand."

She stood and hugged me again, making the soothing sounds. She kissed the top of my head. "I understand. I believe you. That would answer the question the Chief hasn't answered for me. How did you end up on the curb if Dylan was already dead?" Her hands smoothed my hair. "You didn't have exposure. You weren't outside in the elements for long."

Her hand soothed down my rat nest of hair. "Lexi, honey. That means that the killer is still out there. Whoever hurt you is still out there." A small smile played at the corner of her lips. "We'll get them. No one hurts my girl," she said and kissed my head again, the words steel. "Nobody."

Chapter Twenty-Five

Tracey came in to check my vitals, followed quickly by Kavitha with a tray.

"The best soft food the hospital has to offer," she said, and removed the cover with a flourish. My stomach rumbled at the soup with overcooked vegetables and rice floating in it. I skipped the orange gelatin.

"Thanks." I picked up a spoon and sipped the broth, stifling a moan. The dark savory broth tasted like heaven.

Tracey, Kavitha, and Zelda took seats around the bed and chatted, occasionally involving me in the conversation. It was good to do normal things, however small. No one brought up Scott or the investigation. The police would want to speak with me soon enough. These ladies, however formidable, couldn't protect me forever.

Since Nakamura recently announced his retirement and was leaving town, Kavitha had decided to run for the position of Coroner. She had already met with the Chief. It was one of the best ideas I had heard in a long time and the whole town was safer already. I dozed in and out, joining the conversation when I could.

"It's all good," Zelda was speaking when I came to. "The school's administrator was more than happy to start the paperwork to let me retire. I had a student teacher last year and he's still looking for a job, so he'll just slip right in." When she noticed I was awake she winked at me.

"But what are you going to do?" Kavitha took a sip

from her water bottle. "Aren't you too young to take retirement?"

Zelda nodded. "It's one of the few things I'm too young for." Laughter rose around the group. "But don't worry about me. I've got savings and will figure something out." She shrugged. "After all the rumors over the years, I think the new admin is relieved to be rid of me."

I smiled. Between the consistent rumors of our love affair and Zelda's off hours activities, rumors were always flying. I rolled my eyes. It wasn't the first time someone thought she and I were more than friends. Likely, it wouldn't be the last.

"And you can focus on getting Miss Lexi here up and running." Tracy stood and squeezed my foot, then traveled up my leg squeezing. It might look like a friend giving a simple leg massage, but she was checking blood flow.

"True. The only issue I have is Nate." Zelda opened her large bag at her feet and pulled out a bag of chicken nuggets. My stomach growled loud enough to bring smiles to everyone's faces.

"Not for a while yet," Kavitha warned. "Your digestive system needs time to recover." She turned to Zelda. "What about Nate? You guys have been together a while now."

Zelda rolled her eyes. "He's upset I'm not in the building with him all day. I can't figure that one since we hardly ever saw each other back then. He's not pleased that I spend most of my time here. He said this situation is—" she held up her fingers for air quotes, "—out of control."

I grunted. He must be on the outs, finally.

"Exactly! No one comes between us." Zelda popped a nugget in her mouth and smiled.

It was wonderful to laugh and be around people. In the basement, I never thought I would appreciate laughter again or have a sense of safety and contentment. The fear that had been with me faded. I dozed off listening to them chat away and my stomach pleasantly full.

I spent the next few days getting ready to leave the hospital. The Foley catheter came out, and I was able to use the bathroom on my own. The first time out of bed, I needed help, but the second time I did it by myself. My meals progressed from soup to something that was supposed to be chicken. I took a shower and washed my hair. I couldn't style or blow dry it and would schedule a salon appointment for that. In fact, as my physician pointed out, it might be a marvelous opportunity for pampering.

On the day I was scheduled to leave the hospital, Kavitha signed the release papers and sent me home with scripts for a sleeping med until the nightmares ended and something for pain as needed. I was scheduled to go to physical therapy and wound care once a week until probably forever.

Tracey wheeled me out to the car and Zelda waited in the driveway. It was odd to be the one in the wheelchair. Tracey and I hugged, and she promised to stop by on her next day off. I didn't feel bad asking her to bring her famous cabbage soup, and she promised she would.

They helped me in the car and Zelda pulled away from the curb. I slipped sunglasses on and smiled. The sun warmed my muscles, and I relaxed against the leather seats. Safe.

"So, I understand you've moved on to solid food, but want me to stop for nachos?" I groaned and closed my eyes. Drool may have leaked from my mouth. Zelda laughed. "I'll take that as a yes."

We did the drive through. My mouth watered from the scent wafting out of the bag in the car. At my house, Zelda helped me inside. I dropped to the couch, breathless from the activity, and took in my surroundings. After my long absence, I anticipated dust an inch thick. The house was spotless.

Zelda brought in my small overnight bag and flowers in several trips. "Chester and Shirley came by and kept the place up. They used the code you gave Chester to make sure it was safe. I think Shirley even beat me to the grocery store for you." Zelda sat on the couch next to me and tucked her legs under her. "Don't be surprised if they check on you regularly. They were at the hospital a few times."

My eyes widened. "Really?" I wiped the tears away with the back of my hand. I needed to stop crying every time Zelda told me something new. She and I hadn't spoken of Scott or my kidnapping again. It hung in the air with expectation between us. I fidgeted with the hem of my sweater.

"Lexi, honey. We need to talk about what happened. It's scary and hard, but it must be done." Her voice was soft. "The police are going to want to talk to you soon."

I swallowed hard and nodded. No one came to the hospital to take a statement. Tracey and Zelda had acted as watchdogs to keep most people away. I needed to heal, but as time passed, the need to question me was imminent.

"The Chief wants to come by and take your statement. And explain things that happened while you were gone." Her gaze wouldn't meet mine. "I can be there. Or someone else. Whatever you want."

I reached for her and patted her arm. "I want you there. Call the Chief, okay?"

She wiped her face with the back of her hand. "Okay."

"We have to stop crying," I said with a laugh.

"I'll call the Chief after we eat," she promised.

We dived into the food. The aroma was amazing, but I ate half of the plate. Zelda finished her burrito and the rest of my nachos.

Zelda cleared her throat. "Also, I didn't want to worry you, but I haven't been able to get a hold of your parents. I've called their cells and sent emails. Nothing. This entire time. I called the police down there for a wellness check, but they didn't find anything."

Fear welled up in me before my brain caught up. I shook my head. "Don't worry. They're on a cruise. I told you, right? And they refuse to pay for a cell or wi-fi. Once they decide to check their phones, they will lose their minds and be on the first flight back."

Zelda threw her head back and laughed. "Probably screaming about their baby the whole way. I can hear your mother now."

I leaned back, full to bursting, when a knock sounded at the front door.

It opened and Chester stuck his head in. "Hey, Lexi. How you doing?" I tried to stand. He waved me back to the couch and Shirley pushed in behind him. "Sit, sit. Don't get up on our account." They came over and gave me a hug.

Shirley handed me a plate of chocolate brownies that looked as good as they smelled—which was pure heaven. "We just wanted to stop by, drop you off a little something, and make sure you got settled. Zelda put our numbers in your phone. You need anything, day or night. You call us."

"That reminds me." Zelda stood and dug through her purse, pulling out my cell phone. "Here you go." She handed the phone to me. Instead of the usual case, it now had a plastic case on a cord. I stared at it dubiously.

Shirley beamed. "So, you can wear it around your neck. Even in the shower."

Part of me balked at the phone on a rope, but it was a brilliant idea. "Thank you," I said genuinely and draped it around my neck.

They said goodbye and after another round of hugs, locked the door behind themselves.

"You must be tired," Zelda examined my face. "Let's wait and call the Chief later."

I shrugged. "I'd like a bath."

Zelda shook her head. "Nope, not until you're fully healed. Too many options for infections. You can take a shower."

"Okay." I didn't think about the basics from Nursing 101. How long would it take for me to get back to normal? Would I ever?

I made it up the stairs with Zelda behind me. I undressed by myself and stood under the hot water until it ran cold. Turning off the water, I dried off, surprised I still had energy. I was slipping into my nightgown when voices carried up from downstairs.

"You shouldn't be here." Zelda's voice was harsh and cold.

The other voice was quieter, softer, and harder to pick up.

"I don't care what you want. You don't know what she wants. I do." Her voice raised, tensed and laced with venom. "She doesn't want you here."

I came down the stairs to see who she was fighting with. My breath caught in my chest when I saw Scott. His arms hung at his side and his body language spoke to diffusing the situation. Not that it did him any good. Few people calmed Zelda down when she was worked up.

"Look, I just want to talk to her. That's it."

"So, you can convince her you weren't involved? I don't fully understand what happened, Scott." Her face was red. "But I'm going to protect her."

"Like you would know what makes sense?" he spat.

"I'm done with this." She crossed her arms over her chest and cocked a hip. "Get out. Now. Or I'll call the police for trespassing."

He shook his head. "I am the police, idiot."

Zelda pulled herself up to her full five foot seven inches and got in his face. "Wearing a badge or carrying a weapon doesn't make you special. Get. Your. Ass. Out. Or I'll throw you out myself."

I started down the stairs, regardless of my fear. I made it two steps when my knees buckled, and I fell on my butt with a loud thump and a small yelp. The shock hurt more than the actual fall, but the sound of my solid ass hitting the wood stairs caused Zelda and Scott to turn.

Embarrassed, I tried to pull myself to standing but didn't get far. My muscles still sore and my energy waned. Zelda flew up the stairs. "Don't move."

Scott was right behind her. My eyes locked on him.

I cowered against the steps. From somewhere far away, an animal whimpered. Scott shoved Zelda aside. She quickly recovered, grabbed the banister and swung her substantial weight into him, knocking him against the wall. Zelda's arms enveloped me and I buried myself in them.

Zelda quietly rocked me. "Don't you see?" she snarled over her shoulder. "Don't you get it?"

The answer was Scott's quiet footsteps leaving the house.

Chapter Twenty-Six

I woke, safely cocooned in blankets with light filtered through the half-open bathroom. Savoring the comfort, I stretched my limbs, appreciating the soreness as a sign I was alive. Several parts of my body still strained and ached. But something tugged at my neck, held me in place.

Anxiety hit—then I remembered the cell phone hanging from my neck like soap on a rope.

I threw back the covers and sat at the side of the bed for several moments—Nursing 101 kicked in—before I tried to stand and bear weight. When I was confident my legs would hold my weight, I walked out of the room and down the stairs. This time, without falling on my ass.

In the living room, the television flickered, volume turned low to a news channel.

On the couch, dozing softly, sat Chester and Shirley. Not wanting to wake them, I moved quietly and filled a glass of water in the kitchen, drained it, and filled it again.

Shirley bustled into the kitchen. "Let me get that for you, honey." She held her hand out for the glass.

I shook my head. "Thanks but I need to do stuff on my own."

Her mouth turned down. "If you're sure. Don't want you doing too much too fast. Come in and have a seat with us. I'll make a snack."

At the mention of food, my stomach grumbled. Shirley guided me into the living room, and I curled up on the loveseat, a blanket across my lap. I dozed off and awoke to a delightful smell. Shirley held a small bowl of brown goo in front of me. I eyed it suspiciously but took it with a thank you. One bite and buttery sweet cream filled my mouth, so thick and sweet I almost moaned. I greedily took another bite. "What is this?"

"My special recipe. Cream of Wheat," Shirley replied with a wink. "Won't find that on the back of any box."

It had to contain at least a stick of butter, a cup of sugar, and who might guess what else. It didn't matter. I finished it and resisted the urge to lick the bowl clean.

Chester snorted awake when a loud commercial came on. He raised his eyebrows at the empty bowls. "Well, the sleeping princess sleeping princess has graced us with her presence." He glanced at Shirley as she spooned the last of her concoction into her mouth with a playful smile. "Wait a minute, did you make Cream of Wheat?"

Shirley slyly nodded. "And you didn't save me any?" He shook his head. "See what I got to deal with?" he teased.

Shirley playfully smacked him on the arm. "Oh hush, I'll make you some when we get home. This is Lexi's."

"Uh huh, I get that." He returned her grin before becoming serious again. "Lex, we need to have a talk about Scott." At the mention of his name, my stomach heaved. Chester continued, "Now, I appreciate you don't want to, but we gotta. He wants to meet you and talk with you."

I shook my head. "Not until I talk with the Chief. I don't fully understand what happened to me or what the police, or anyone else, thinks happened. But I want to learn the truth, and I can't have Scott in the middle of things right now."

Chester considered it and nodded. "That's not a bad idea." He gestured upstairs. "Zelda's up in the guest room in case you were wondering."

I smiled, knowing she wouldn't have gone very far. "She okay?"

Shirley replied, "She's all good, honey. We came in right after you passed out on the stairs. Separated those two fools before they did any damage." Shirley laughed. "They both love you something fierce."

"We're goin' to be monitoring this house for a while. Just to make sure you okay. We don't have anything else to do," he finished with a laugh.

Shirley gently smacked him. "Man, please! Really though, Lex, don't be walking around nude in front of the windows. We don't want to be seeing nothing."

I joined in their laughter and promised I wouldn't. We sat on the couch and talked and dozed until sunrise, when they said they had to get to the coffee house. Every morning, a group of retirees met for coffee and breakfast and to see who died. Shirley and Chester had to get there before folks started writing their obituaries. I waved as they closed the door and set the alarm behind themselves.

Instead of staying up, I made my way back to bed and curled under the blankets. The weather was cool and overcast, perfect for sleeping. The trees were bare now, and the first days of winter had arrived. I fell into a deep sleep fast. Full sun woke me sometime later. I stretched, and made my way downstairs, more stable and stronger.

Zelda bustled around the kitchen, dressed and making breakfast. I slipped into a seat at the island and watched her fish waffles out of the waffle maker with a fork before drowning them with maple syrup.

"Good morning," Zelda said, adding bacon to her plate. "Looks like you got up and cooked last night?" she inquired with a raised eyebrow.

"No, Shirley," I answered and stole a piece of bacon from her plate. "Best cream of wheat ever."

"Ewww, glad I missed that. How are you feeling? Sore?"

"I don't think I'll ever not be sore. What happened between you and Scott?"

Zelda popped in a mouthful of waffle and chewed slowly. "He wanted to talk to you, and I wouldn't let him near you. When you saw him in the hospital, you practically lost your mind. Last night wasn't much better." She speared a waffle hard enough to scrap the plate. "I'm not letting that happen again."

"I'll meet with him." Zelda opened her full mouth to interrupt, but I gave her a look that stopped her. "But not until I talk to the Chief. I want the actual truth. My memories, my experiences, are valid. I have to make sense of them and what the official truth is. I have to know before I can talk to Scott. But I will have to talk with him eventually."

Zelda's gaze searched my face for a moment before she nodded. "I'll text the Chief and let him know." The waffle machine dinged, and she opened the lid to pull another off. "Until then, waffles?"

My stomach grumbled again, and I dug into the plate she put before me. It wasn't as good as Shirley's cream of wheat, but close.

****

A few days later, I felt better and stronger. Zelda had set up a meeting with Chief Wagner. He offered to come to my house, but I declined. It was hard enough living with the scars and pain every minute. I didn't want to relive the torture and trauma in my living room. Zelda drove me to the station and waited at the front desk with Nakamura's son. It looked like he stayed around, even if his dad didn't.

The Chief stood in his office doorway, concern etched his brows and deep frown. "Lexi, honey, how are you?" He wrapped me in a warm bear hug. This was the man I grew up with, not the hardened law officer.

I returned his hug. "Doing better every day."

"Have a seat, honey." He motioned to the familiar chair, and I took the chair opposite his desk. "Look, Lexi. I wanted to speak with you for a couple of reasons. We need to get your statement. Officer Davis can take that. We also need to talk about what happened while you were... gone." He waved his hands dismissively. "The official events, not what you might hear from others."

My mind went to the darkness, pain, slashing, the animal smell mixed with Scott's cologne. I had to drag myself out of the memories before I responded. "I understand, but I don't know what I can tell you that the scene can't."

His frown deepened. "That's the thing, actually one of several things we to clear up. We haven't been able to find the house where you were held. Now, I realize you're hurt and held captive, no doubt about that." He shook his head, his glaze far away. "But where? Let's take your statement and go over stuff."

I nodded. They weren't looking at Scott's house. I

would give my statement and they would take down what I said. But Scott wasn't an idiot. He'd clean the place, but probably miss a speck of something. That's how it always happened in the movies.

Officer Harris brought with him the heavy scent of drug store body spray and hair gel. As he balanced the laptop on his knees, I wondered if he had started shaving yet. But he was professional as he took my statement, pausing when I became overwhelmed. He didn't rush me but did ask questions to clarify certain points. When I mentioned it was Scott who held me captive, the Chief and Harris exchanged a glance, but nothing was said.

When it was completed, the Chief slipped off his glasses and rubbed the bridge of his nose. "I'm awful sorry this happened to you, Lex." He exhaled hard. "I need some coffee. Want some coffee? Water? Soda?"

I chose soda, and he left the room in a hurry behind the officer. Alone, I stood and stretched my arms overhead. The physical therapist didn't want me sitting for more than an hour at a time. I didn't have the heart to tell him even before the accident I could sit for hours on end, especially if the streaming series was good. I'd keep that to myself.

The Chief came back in with a cold can of soda. I sipped the sugary liquid and sighed. Small pleasures in life had gained new significance.

He took his seat and slurped his coffee. "Now, I'd like to talk about what happened while you were in the hospital. When Scott tried to visit you?" He took another sip of coffee and glanced over the rim at me.

I took a deep breath; my hands tightened so hard on the icy can, the aluminum bent. "It was him, Chief. I know it. He's the one that kidnapped me."

He opened his mouth to speak, but I shook my head and stopped him. My mind raced with a hundred reasons it was Scott. I couldn't name all of them fast enough. "No, let me talk." I swallowed down the knot in my throat to continue. "I smelled his cologne every time he came into the room to do this." I held up my arms with the stitches scabbing over but still visible for his inspection. He glanced down at the mug. "The police radio was on constantly upstairs. The laundry area was in the same spot as in his house. It's his house, Chief. The window had those little bars on it. Same as his house."

The silence sat heavily between us. The Chief folded his hands on the desk and leaned into them. His shoulders dropped with defeat. "I don't know what to tell you. What you're saying makes it sound like Scott. It really does. But I know for a fact it can't be. He was out searching for you. I don't think he got more than a couple of hours of sleep during those weeks. And most of it was on the couch in his office." The Chief's fingers intertwined tight enough to turn the knuckles white. "I hear you and I believe you. I just don't see how it could be Scott."

I cleared my throat of the thickness threatening to choke me. "Go to his house, search it. There has to be evidence of something."

Chief Wagner leaned back in the chair and rocked it. "I'm leery of doing that. Not that I don't trust you. I do. I really do. It's just in a small town like this if neighbors witness a solid member of the police force's house being gone through or if word got out of the search warrant... well, we have a hard enough time getting people to trust us after everything that's happened in the world. It might make the situation worse."

Dumbfounded, my head spun. "You're more worried about how things look than the truth? That's how I got kidnapped in the first place. If you all had been honest about Buffy's death, I wouldn't have had to investigate it." My words were high-pitched and hysterical. I bit my cheek to keep from saying more. This was their fault, and one of their own had hurt me.

"Now, wait a minute. There's no hiding anything. There was an ongoing investigation. One, I might add, you and that friend of yours almost derailed many times. If anything, you're the reason Celeste Stewart and Dylan Condor are dead. Now, more victims won't have closure." He took a deep breath and held it before exhaling. "Lex, I don't want to point fingers here, but you are part of the problem."

"So, I deserved what happened to me?" My voice choked. My breath wouldn't come.

He stumbled over words, struggling to find the right ones. "No, not at all. I'm saying I can't and won't investigate Scott. He has an outstanding record as a law enforcement officer. On any force. Not one complaint in almost twenty years in service. Myself even, I've had several complaints over the years."

I blinked hard to fight back the tears and willed my hand not to wipe my eyes. All I could do was nod.

"Lex, honey. I can't understand what you went through or what you have to deal with now. But I swear on my children and grandkids, it wasn't Scott who did this."

I sensed his gaze bored into me, but I couldn't meet it. His position was obvious.

"And you really think we caused the deaths?" My

heart broke at the idea that Zelda and I had caused Celeste's death. She was difficult but was a kind soul. I couldn't stop my bottom lip from quivering and finally gave in and the tears flowed.

"Now, Lex, don't... I... here's some tissues." He handed me a box of tissues from the corner of the desk.

I took several and wiped my face and eyes. I sniffed and straightened my back. If I let it, the wave of despair would carry me away on rough rapids of pain and I'd never come up for air. "Sorry," I whispered.

"No, no. Don't be. It's a hard situation. Any way you look at it. Have you talked to the doctor yet?"

"Which one?" I shook my head. "Wound care, physical therapy, the therapist to make sure I'm still sane after everything or a plain old medical doctor? My schedule is full of medical appointments lately."

His brow furrowed; his voice remained gentle. "I understand Dylan gave you some drugs. Do you think that may be part of it? Maybe what you remember is the effects of the drugs twisting things.

"I've heard of things like that happening." Drugs and medications of any type had different reactions to different people. It's not impossible that some of what I had experienced was drug-induced. "But I know what I experienced, and it wasn't all drugs."

"Are you talking to a professional therapist? You've been through a lot."

I nodded again. "Yes, starting tomorrow. Zelda wants me to only do one appointment a day, so I don't wear myself out."

"She's a good friend, takes good care of you." He sighed. "I hope I didn't hurt you when I said you all caused those deaths. I lost my temper, and I shouldn't have."

I remembered too well how quickly he could lose his temper from when I was on the soccer field as a kid. Back then I thought it was passion, now it was the traits of a bully out of touch with his emotions. I wanted to believe he was still one of the good guys but like so much recently, I realized he wasn't.

He continued. "Chances are extremely high that Dylan would have committed those crimes. What I don't understand is why he didn't go after Neveah."

"She's okay?" I had asked at the hospital, but no one had the information.

"Yeah, she's good. We did a wellness check on her after we found Celeste. She was scared, but okay."

"I should go visit her." I held up both hands. "As a friend, nothing more."

The Chief laughed. "She'd probably like that, but she left town." When he recognized the surprise on my face, he continued. "Really left town. Confirmed. She went to cosmetology school in the city. Staying with an aunt down there. I have a buddy on the Kansas City force who agreed to check up on her periodically."

My heart lifted. Something good came out of all of this. "Wow, that's great."

The Chief and I did some small talk about his family and plans to visit the grandkids, maybe even his retirement. I agreed to make sure I would attend the party whenever it was. We hugged when I left the office. I didn't have the answers I wanted, but now I wasn't sure I wanted them.

Chapter Twenty-Seven

Zelda walked with me to the car, not commenting on my red eyes and smeared makeup. I mumbled something and put my seat belt on.

"You okay? Was he mean?" Zelda had never played soccer under the Chief, preferring to read instead of participating in sports, but Wagner the coach had a reputation.

"Not really. He said we may have caused Celeste's death and then apologized." I stopped, waiting for her reaction. Her eyes widened and her jaw swung open. "He won't investigate Scott, said it looks bad for the department and the case is closed."

Her mouth fell further open, her jaw hanging. "Same shit, different day."

We sat in the car for a few moments while Zelda and I stared at each other until she laughed and closed her mouth.

"For a moment there, I thought you were going to catch flies." I joined her, laughing.

"About to. He did nothing, absolutely nothing?"

"He took my statement." I shrugged. In the sunlight and outside openness, it seemed the best response. The entire exchange seemed surreal. "From the note in his pocket, Dylan confessed to all the crimes. We can go back to our normal lives."

Zelda clicked her tongue and put the car in gear,

backing out of the space. "No, I'm not going back to my normal life." She made her fingers into air quotes at the end. "I'm not sure about investigating stuff, but I also don't want to go back to the classroom." She put the car in Drive and headed to my house.

We stumbled more than anything while during the investigation, that might not be where our future was headed. But the long hours, ungrateful patients and, annoying physicians no longer interested me.

She pulled into the driveway and parked. I exhaled hard, not wanting to have the conversation that waited. "Zel, I'd like to be alone."

She shook her head like I knew she would. "I don't think that's a good idea."

"I realize that, but I still want some time to myself. I promise to wear the phone and check in regularly." I was pleading like a teenager trying to stay out after curfew.

Zelda propped her arm on the door ledge and dropped her forehead into her hand. We sat and she chewed her lip. "Fine. I get it. I just worry about you." Her voice quivered. "I don't want to experience life without you. For weeks, I had to imagine that and I don't want to think of it ever again."

I reached across the car and hugged her tight. Zelda had the biggest heart to go along with the biggest mouth. It was what made her special. And occasionally dangerous. I released her and moved back into my seat. "I promise I'll check in."

Zelda sniffed and wiped her eyes. "Right. You're checking in every even hour," her voice stern.

I frowned. "That's a bit much, Zel. How about every four hours and when I go to bed, like ten-ish?"

She stared at me a long time, debating whether to fight me. I said a silent prayer she wouldn't. If she did, she would win. Finally, she gave in. "Okay, but if you miss one call or text, I'm calling the police and breaking down your door."

I hugged her again and laughed. "Don't worry, I'll go inside, turn the alarm on, and text you. My plan is to lie down and relax. It's all good."

Inside, I set the alarm immediately and dropped my tote bag by the door. I kicked off my shoes and stood in the small foyer. An empty house to yourself contained a different type of silence than an occupied house. In the kitchen, I grabbed cheese, crackers, and a drink and ate it on the kitchen island. I savored the stillness of home. No machines beeping, no murmur of voices or televisions. Nothing but the hum of the refrigerator and cars going by outside.

Before I forgot, I texted Zelda a quick "I'm fine" message.

A crawling sensation spread across my skin. I clenched my fist to resist the urge to scratch. Upstairs, I grabbed the prescription cream and rubbed it over my wounds. In the bathroom, under the luminous light, I inspected the injuries. I would either have to learn to live with the scars or have a crap ton of plastic surgery.

The mirror reflected the beginnings of crow's feet at the corner of my eyes but otherwise, I was aging well. It never bothered me, and plastic surgery hadn't been on my radar. One more thing to add to the list of things I never thought I would have to deal with. I changed into jogger pants and a hoodie and curled up on the couch with my cell phone around my neck as I promised Zelda. I clicked over to a streaming service and settled on a museum heist documentary and snuggled in.

The documentary kept my attention, but my body ached, and my heart suffered. I threw the blanket off and walked to the window and stared out. The world outside didn't seem as bright as it once did. Had I only seen the childhood memories and not the real world? I shook my head. So far, my leave of absence was indefinite, and it would be permanent. I needed time to see the world through healed eyes.

A decision made, I grabbed my laptop and typed out my resignation letter. Several minutes later, I finished it and I didn't pause before hitting send to human resources. A weight lifted off my chest. I debated about texting Zelda. No, I'd wait until the assigned time. It would give us something to talk about. It had been years, decades, since I thought about doing anything other than nursing. I shook my head and smiled. The future was unsettled, but whatever it held, it would be good things. I would make sure of it. Coming close to death made me want only good things around me.

My soul lifted but my body unable to rest and mind unfocused, I turned to the local news. The lead story was the local spelling bee winner that moved on to the county spelling bee. The kid had a long way to go to be the national winner, but from the newscaster's level of excitement, the kid was a shoe in. The optimism gave me hope. Good always won over evil.

Far into the newscast, after the weather teaser, was a follow-up on the Werewolf Murders as they were now called. They showed individual photos of Buffy and Celeste. My eyes teared up seeing smiling happy photos from better days for the ladies. When the photo of Dylan popped up, my breath caught in my throat. I hadn't seen a full body photo of him. Most of the photos on his social media were from the chest up with a girl tucked under his arm. The full body photo showed a slim figure. Slight was too generous. Dylan was a reed, lanky, with slim hips. Costumes could hide a body, but this wasn't the same man I saw running from my house or held me hostage for weeks. Whoever wore the costume appeared thicker, more solid. But it couldn't have been Scott either. He didn't have a beer belly or carry an extra ten pounds of weight. Whoever had worn the costume was bigger, more meaty than Scott or Dylan.

I lifted the phone to call Zelda, but my hand stopped short of it. The promise she made in the hospital to find the real killer had been forgotten, never brought up again. But I knew she would want to know this. I texted her.

—Hey, did you see photos of Dylan? I don't think he's the killer. I know, but listen, whoever wore the costume seemed fatter around the middle. Dylan is a bean pole. Scott's not too far off. The actual killer is still out there—.

I hit send and exhaled hard. After weeks in captivity, endless days in the hospital, and months of rehab to look forward to, the killer was still out there. We might never sort this out.

I stared at the phone, willing Zelda to text me back. Frustrated and filled with nervous energy, I debated about going for a walk. I hadn't been outside my myself yet. The idea didn't scare me, and I took that as a good sign. I threw on a light jacket, grabbed keys, set the alarm again and headed out.

The sun was already behind the trees this late in the afternoon, throwing low shadows across the street.

Leaves had fallen, leaving the trees bare and an icy wind rustled the empty branches. The air chilled my skin, and it didn't take long for my breathing to become heavy and labored. I stopped, putting my hands on my hips and struggled to fill my lungs. A dull pain grew on my side. Not sharp, but reason to be concerned. I turned around and headed home. The ding from my chest grabbed my attention. Zelda returned my text.

—Okay, I love you. Let this crap go. Let's focus on Bora Bora or something where we can get drinks brought to us by gorgeous men in speedos—.

She finished the text with a winky face emoji to soften her words. Bora Bora? We'd talked about Hawaii, not Bora Bora. I moved considerably slower, and my muscles ached. Knowing Zelda, she probably had moved on to Bora Bora and had neglected to mention it. Back at the house, I turned off the alarm and locked the door behind me, resetting the alarm. I could do Hawaii, but Bora Bora sounded a bit advanced for someone who hadn't taken a real vacation in years.

—Okay. Let's pull back on Bora Bora and focus on Hawaii, Okay? One tropical destination at a time. Lol—
.

I made myself dinner and ate, occasionally checking the phone. No further response from Zelda. Her feelings must have been hurt, and I made a mental note to call her tomorrow. I thought I wanted the time away, but it was weird not having someone at my side. When the phone finally dinged, I smiled, expecting it to be Zelda bitching about something.

Instead, it was Scott. My heart tugged in my throat.

Chapter Twenty-Eight

—Heard you talked to the Chief. Can I come over? I'd like to talk.—

Exhaustion made my bones ache but I wanted to wrap things up with him. And apologize. It was the right thing to do. Endings were important.

—Sure, come on over. I don't want to fight.—

The three dots indicated him texting back was immediate.

—I promise, no fighting. Just want to talk.—

I gave his text a thumbs up and dropped the phone around my neck. I cleaned up the kitchen and tidied the living room. He usually made it to my house in fifteen minutes—that was if he was at his house when he texted. My phone dinged again. Time to take medication.

The knock at the door and alarm app sounded at the same time. I checked the camera to see Scott standing on the doorstep waving at the camera. I opened the door with a small smile. He held a box from my favorite bakery in town. "You could use some sugary goodness."

I took the box happily. "Come in." I held the door open and locked it behind him. "Do you want one?"

He patted his non-existent belly. "No thanks. I might have had a few already." He laughed. "Need to keep my slim figure."

I let my eyes travel down his body. He couldn't have been inside that costume. There was no doubt he wasn't the one that hurt me. I motioned him to take a seat and put the box of goodies on the island before taking a seat next to him on the couch.

"Look," Scott started. "I wanted to wrap things up." He chuckled softly. "That sounds harsh, doesn't it? Like it's a business deal or something." His gaze fell to the floor.

I tucked my legs loosely under myself and tried to exude a sense of calm. Again, my fingers found the hem of my sweatshirt and played with a loose thread. "I realize a lot has happened." I wanted to reach out and pat his hand. Instead, I squeezed mine into a fist.

"At least you didn't scream when I walked in the door." He was trying to lighten the mood. Scott always told awkward jokes when he was anxious.

"Yeah, I have to apologize for that. When I was kidnapped, everything I experienced told me you were the person who hurt me. All of my memories said you did this to me." I held out my arms to him. His face darkened when his gaze fell on the scabs and red marks. "It wasn't you, and I'm sorry." I stopped talking and bit my cheek. The words left a foreign taste in my mouth.

His gaze met mine, eyes wide. "Really? You're sorry?"

"It's not enough. It never can be. I can't take those words back. But I am sorry. At the time, I was certain it was you with every fiber of my being."

My voice drifted off. I had hurt him and falsely accused him of a crime. There was nothing I can do to make it better. Only time would do that. And distance.

He nodded; gaze adverted. "I shouldn't have been harsh with you. I'm sorry. It wasn't my intention. I hoped you'd give it up, but I should have known you better.

Hell, I should have paid more attention all along."

Tears started at the corner of my eyes. "There were more issues than not paying attention."

We sat in silence, our breathing and the wind outside the only sounds. "Maybe another time, things might be different." Scott's voice broke and he quickly cleared his throat with a cough.

I vigorously nodded. So much to say but no words came. "Another time." A nervous laugh escaped me.

Scott reached over and squeezed my hand. "Another time, another life."

The conversation had to change, or I would reach my arms out to him and welcome him back. A question that had been bothering me that I had to ask. "Did Zelda and I really derail the investigation?"

A small smile played at the corner of his lips, and he shook his head. "No, nor did you cause Celeste's death. In fact, there's evidence that Dylan had tried to get to her earlier, but your visits delayed his plan. We think he thought you all had her under surveillance. And your involvement kept it in the Chief's eye. You did good." He patted my hand, gently. "You usually do."

"Seeing all the corruption and half ass attitude during this, I had to get to the truth. I had to get closure." The knot in my throat stopped me from saying more.

"That's the hardest thing in law enforcement. Most of the time, we never get closure." He shook his head. "When I was on patrol, I would go to a call and never see the outcome. I can't tell you the number of domestic calls I wondered what happened to the people, to the kids. Give up needing that closure. You do the best you can."

"What do you know about the Chief appointing someone as coroner?" I asked, clearing my throat.

"Word travels fast, uh?" He chuckled softly. "I don't know what he has in mind, but he'll appoint someone in the next month to hold over until the next election. Not a big rush." He eyed me curiously. "You considered applying?"

I sat still for a moment. The idea hadn't occurred to me. "No, Kavitha is."

He shook his head. "She's good but you'd be a good candidate, too. It doesn't pay much. That was part of the issue with Nakamura. He expected more than the county could provide."

"Is that why he half assed stuff?"

He nodded. "Possibly. I hate to say it, but sometimes he wouldn't even examine the bodies. He'd just sign off on whatever the attending physician told him or wrote in the chart. Hell, one time I saw him sign off on what the Chief said. It rubbed me wrong."

I nodded. It rubbed me wrong, too. "He wasn't giving the remains the respect they deserved. That bothered me."

The small talk dwindled until there was nothing left to say between us. We exchanged pleasantries and a warm hug at the door. As Scott walked down the sidewalk to his car he turned around. Our eyes met and I would have sworn his eyes were moist When he turned away finally, the hand that wiped his face confirmed it.

Chapter Twenty-Nine

Every day, I got stronger. My wounds healed but there would be scaring. The idea of plastic surgery came and went. Zelda and I finalized our trip to Hawaii. We ordered swimsuits online and had a try on party with a couple bottles of wine and chicken wings.

Zelda was vetoing a swimsuit when my phone rang. My parents finally found free Wi-Fi. I swiped on the facetime option and held the phone in front of me. "Hey, Mom."

Zelda quickly hid the half-empty bottle of wine under suits and scooted into the frame next to me. "Hi, Miss Kay. How's the cruise?"

My mom's out-of-control gray curls filled the screen. "Ugh, so many people. Everywhere. And your father has to talk to all of them. Who knew there were so many islands in the world? And so much water, I know people say the planet is mostly water but *oy vey.*" She pushed her face against the screen. "Is that Zelda? Zelda?"

Zelda and I swallowed laughter. "Hi, Miss Kay." Zelda waved enthusiastically.

From somewhere in the background, my father said, "Kay, you don't need to be that close for heaven's sake. The girls don't need to see your sunburn."

My mom pulled back and threw a death glare over her shoulder. "Fine. Lexi, honey, how are you? Zelda said you were on death's door. You look fine."

I kept my gaze on the screen as Zelda smacked my leg out of frame. "I was in the hospital for a bit but I'm doing better. Nothing to worry about."

My mom's knowing stare pierced through the screen. "Uh hu. I'll be the judge of that –"

"If the woman says she's fine, she's fine. Let her live, Kay!"

My mom's eyes rolled back in their sockets. "For hell's sake, Manny. No one asked you. Go find someone to talk to."

Zelda and I couldn't contain our laughter and it spilled out. My parents were coming up on their fifty-wedding anniversary. If they didn't argue, they would have long divorced. The idea that Scott and I should have argued more occurred to me and I shoved it aside as quickly. For now.

My mom's lips pressed together in disapproval. "I'll be the judge of whether you're fine or not. We're leaving the cruise at the next port and heading back to Atherton. Of course, it'll take us several days as we're in the middle of the Indian Ocean."

"I have an idea. We're going to Hawaii in a couple weeks. Why don't you meet us there?" Zelda asked, too sweetly. It was my turn to smack her leg. She continued. "Three weeks on two islands. Beach front rentals. I've researched restaurants and planned activities every day."

"Hmmm…. we can't stay the whole time, but it would be easier to get off in Sydney and catch a flight." Mom banged her hand on the table, dropping the phone.

The phone fumbled and my parents argued about whether it was broken and if they had enough sun block medications to go to Hawaii and if I would survive that long without them. Zelda and I waited patiently for them to right the phone. Now, my dad held the phone at arm's length and his smile lit the screen. "Lexi, *bubbeleh*. We will meet you in Hawaii. Zelda, send me an email with all the details. Okay? We can't wait to see you two!"

"Can't wait to see you both," I said, less excited. We exchanged goodbyes and assurances that I indeed was alive and would continue living until they saw me. When the call finally ended five minutes later, I dropped the phone with a groan.

"Did you have to invite them to Hawaii?" It's supposed to be relaxing."

Zelda playfully smacked me on the leg and pulled out the bottle of wine. "It seemed like a good idea."

I made a face. "Do you know how many of your ideas seem like a good idea?"

She poured a glass and stuck out her tongue at me. "I can't help it if the universe guides us to interesting situations."

"If that's what you want to call it." I grabbed a swimsuit and started to change. I turned the conversation to men. "What's going on with you and Nate?"

She and I spent more time together than usual. If we weren't together, we called or texted about the trip. It was her way of keeping tabs on me without it being obvious, or so she thought. I hadn't heard a word about Nate or their relationship.

Her face scrunched up in distaste. "I cut him loose. You called it. He controlled everything." She shrugged. "He lost his shit recently, and it was more than slightly disturbing."

I raised my eyebrows. I hadn't heard this. "What happened?" I slipped on a two-piece suit and stood in front of the mirror in shock. When my hip cocked more showed than was decent. "I need a bikini wax ASAP."

Zelda rolled her eyes. "Whatever, no one cares what your cooch looks like. And if they're looking that closely, they're either interested in it or need to mind their business."

I laughed. "Okay, my cooch aside, what about Nate? What did he do that was disturbing?" The suit looked good. I shimmied in place and felt my old self coming back. The suit was a keeper. As long as I didn't put my hip out too far.

Zelda stretched out on my bed, a frown on her face. "Remember when you needed alone time?" Her fingers curled in air quotes. I nodded. "He'd been bugging me for weeks to make me dinner, but I was always busy. Anyways, he came over, brought dinner. Candles, china plates, all of it. He's over the top, I used to find it endearing but…whatever." She sat up and gazed at the floor and fidgeted with a suit. "He laid it all out and expected me to be wowed'. I guess I wasn't as into it as he wanted me to be."

I slipped out of the suit and picked out another. "He got mad? That you weren't excited?"

She nodded, still staring at the floor. "Yeah. Like a rage. I had never seen him like that. I thought for sure he would hurt me." She hugged herself and rubbed her hands up and down her arms. "He started screaming and throwing the plates, food flew everywhere. Plates shattered."

I stopped trying on suits and sat next to her on the bed, giving her time to finish. "Did he hurt you?"

She sniffed hard. "You know I move fast when I need to." Her gaze met mine, and she laughed. She had a way of avoiding stuff. Not a skill I possessed, clearly. "I couldn't get him to calm down. He raged like an animal. I threatened to call the police, even had the phone in my hand, and he went completely still. He just stood there. Like he wasn't even breathing." She fell quiet, back in that moment of terror. "Then he just walked out." She shrugged. "I tried to call him, I even texted him but no response."

"Were you guys talking about anything disturbing or something that would frustrate him, or did it come out of nowhere because you weren't impressed?" Zelda knew how to push buttons on people without realizing. Like a sixth sense to get your ass kicked.

Tears welled in her eyes. "I've racked my brain trying to figure out what I could have done."

I reached out and rubbed her back. "You did nothing to deserve that behavior. I didn't mean to imply that. Sorry."

She slumped against me. This was Zelda's gentle heart she didn't let people see. Probably the best part of her. I was lucky to know it. "I know. And I shouldn't have given it two thoughts. But I did." She shrugged and wiped a hand across her face, removing tears and sniffing. "But I can't stop wondering what happened."

Scott's words came back to me as I rubbed Zelda's back. "Sometimes you have to get used to not getting answers or closure."

"Yeah, that's not something I'm good at, but I get it." She slipped off the bed and started undressing to try on a suit. "It's been a couple of weeks and it still doesn't sit well with me."

I slipped off the suit and tried on another. Zelda looked ridiculously good in the one she tried on. And she certainly wasn't concerned about bikini waxes. "So, you haven't seen him or heard from him? He's not even tried to reach out?" Nate's relationship style always seemed suffocating. It seemed odd he wasn't contacting her.

She shook her head and posed in front of the mirror, throwing a hip to one side. "Not a word. Nothing. This suit is pretty cute." The red halter-style one piece ruched in at the waist. She looked like a pin-up with her curly hair framing her face.

"You'll turn heads for sure in that." This one piece wasn't a winner. It crushed my boobs and did nothing for my stomach that had grown during my time off. "Are you worried he'll do something dangerous? Because didn't you think he was following you at one point?"

"Eh, no? He always talked game but didn't come through with it. But there was something…off about him. I never could put my finger on it." She nodded at the suit in approval and slipped it off, picking through the others with a frown. "How many did you say I needed?"

"We need three suits, minimum." I tried another one and liked the look of it. The two-piece bandera top looked like lingerie with bits of see-through mesh. The bottom curved nicely on my butt and didn't cut too high on the front. No need for wax with this one. "This is a keeper."

Zelda turned an approving eye to me. "Agreed." She threw a suit down on the bed and reached for her clothes. "I'm tried out. I've got two good ones."

"Agreed. I'll return the others." I slipped the suit off and put on my regular clothes. "I'll see if there're any others I can find."

"Okay," Zelda exhaled hard. "I've got to go by the

school and get a few things from my classroom."

"You're done, then?" I asked, warily.

"Yep, the teacher who took over is great. I'm giving them most of the things from the classroom. There are just a few things I keep forgetting to go pick up that I want."

"You've really given it all up?" Were we really starting a new chapter of our lives?

"Yep. I loved teaching, but it's time to move on. And I'm not giving anything up. New adventures," she said with a wink.

Zelda and I finished dressing and packing up the swimsuits to mail back. We were wrapping stuff up when the doorbell rang. I frowned. The front door camera hadn't notified me of someone at the door. I shrugged and made a mental note to check the settings.

Downstairs, the doorbell rang again, insistent. "Hold your horses, I'm coming." I shouted across the living room. More than likely it was Shirley and Chester being polite and not using their key.

Zelda stood behind me going through her purse when I opened the door. Nate stood there in his usual uniform of a purple silk shirt, faded black jeans, and aged combat boots. A wide smile spread on his face that didn't reach his glassy eyes.

A long, wicked looking knife rested in one in his hand.

He growled, the sound deep and rumbling out of his chest.

Chapter Thirty

Zelda shrieked, but it died in her throat. Nate shut the door then and pushed past me into the room. I stood frozen against the wall as his gaze leered over each of us in turn. The heavy scent of Scott's cologne hit me. My breath caught in my throat.

He strolled to stand in front of Zelda, towering over her. "I tried to get both of you to pull the stick out of your asses and go back to your boring lives." A sarcastic laugh tumbled from his mouth. "Go back to your boring ass lives and leave everything alone. Just couldn't do it, could you?"

Something like a squeak escaped Zelda. I remained against the wall, my muscles tense and frozen.

He sat on the couch and crossed one leg over the other. One arm draped casually across the back, the other resting on his leg. Light reflected off the blade resting against the faded denim jeans. "Why don't you come have seats with me?" A smile played at the corner of his lips. He acted like he was there for a game night or dinner. His casualness froze me.

I took in Nate's thick midsection, straining against the shiny fabric. His build matched the person in the costume.

Zelda and I locked gazes. I attempted to send her a silent message. "*He's the guy. It's him.*"

"Get your asses over here!" Nate's scream loosened

my bowels.

Zelda moved to join me on the loveseat. "Now, Zellie baby. Come sit with me." Nate patted the couch cushion next to him. "I have a surprise for you."

Zelda's eyes widened before sliding onto the couch as far from him as possible. It took every ounce of willpower to sit on the loveseat. We were only feet apart, but it felt like miles.

"Good girls, good girls." He ran a hand through his greasy hair. "That wasn't so hard, was it? Now, we're going to have a little chat. If I don't like how it goes, I'll tear you to shreds." His voice was quiet and unnervingly gentle.

My fingers found a seam Shirley repaired on the loveseat cushion and frantically traced it. "You...'"

Everything about Nate screamed something removed from reality.

"What?" Zelda's head spun from me to Nate, gaze wide-eyed. "Oh, my God. You!. You hurt her." The color left her face. "You did it. All of it."

Nate's eyebrows wiggled playfully, and he tilted his head back, shaking his shoulder length hair. "I most certainly did. I played with you like a kid with a new toy. I had you running around town chasing your own asses. You both fell for it. But you especially, Zellie baby. You fell for it hard."

Zelda's hand gripped her stomach, and a groan escaped her. "Oh, God... no."

He winked, his eyes dead, and blew her a kiss. "Remember what we did the night the news hit of Buffy's death?" The light from a table lamp glinted off the metal blade in his hand. My other hand found another seam and furiously rubbed it.

Zelda bolted for the half bath. Her retching carried through the open door to where we sat.

A cold sweat washed over me. "Why? Why did you do this to me? To us?"

Nate's smile never faltered. "Because." He tapped the crossed leg to an imaginary beat. "Because you always make it about you. She always makes it about you. I thought I'd take you, have some fun. But Zelda wouldn't leave it alone, out on the streets everyday, looking for you. Hell, she even went to Kansas City, searching the hospitals and morgues for your body. She would never really be mine. That's when I realized I had to end both of you but first I would destroy you."

"You let me go to kill us both?"

Nate winked and his lips twitched. "Smart, right? I must say, I have this criminal life down."

The toilet flushed and water ran from the sink. "Zellie baby don't get any ideas now. Come on back here."

She shuffled into the room and dropped next to me. Her eyes were red and watery, face pale and blotchy.

"Let's get back to what you and I did that night." His tone sounded almost sensual. My stomach retched. "More like what did you do that night? You know I could still smell the girl's blood while we—?"

Zelda shook next to me and buried her head in my shoulder. All of her strength seeped out of her. Never had I seen her like this. Her weakness terrified me more than Nate or the blade. My hope faltered.

"Do you remember, Zellie babe? I remember your tongue sliding down my—"

"Stop it!" Zelda screamed. I recoiled at her pain. "Just stop it." Her voice dissolved in tears. My arm tightened around her.

Nate snickered. My heart pounded in my head. The chance of survival was rock bottom. This man had manipulated Zelda and me and the town was convinced the crimes had been committed by someone else. Hell, it wasn't that long ago I was convinced it was Scott.

"Scott's cologne, the radio...all of it was to mess with me, wasn't it?"

"Just a bit of fun. I wish I had been there when you woke up in the hospital and lost it." His belly giggled. "I bet it was a sight." The laughter rolled out of him and punched into me. Each one bruised the scarred, still healing wounds.

However long I lived I never wanted to hear that sound again. "I have something for you." He lifted his hips and reached into his front jeans pocket, the knife still firmly in his hand. "A gift. Something I've been keeping just for you. Special."

I didn't want to stare but I couldn't tear my eyes away from his hand. From his pocket, he pulled out a cell phone. The cover was pink and black glitter with hearts and knives. Something about it was childish. He held the phone out and wiggled it. "Know what this is?"

I wanted to answer sarcastically and take him down a few pegs, but my mouth wouldn't open.

"Zellie baby, you're the smart one here. What is this? Want to guess?" Nate shook the phone again and raised his eyes in question. No answer came from Zelda. "No?" He clicked his tongue. "I'm so disappointed in you. Any whoo, this is a cell phone."

He brought the phone to his face and pretended to examine it, like he'd never seen one before. "I got this, well, picked it up really, from one of my...let's say sacrificial lambs?" He chuckled low. "Wanna take a look?" He tossed the phone at Zelda.

It hit her, then bounced to the carpet. But not before the lock screen lit up. On the screen was a picture of a teenage girl on a merry-go-round smiling, blonde hair streaming behind her.

I bent to pick it up. "Buffy?"

"You recognize her? I thought I'd left her changed. So, to speak." His lips quivered like it was the funniest thing he'd ever said.

I picked it up and held it to my chest. "Why do you have her phone?"

Nate shrugged. "To cover my ass. We'd been talking and those were conversations I did not want the police to see. Shit, the texts alone would land me in jail."

My head throbbed and my face flushed red. "You were messing with her?"

"Not right away. But I was planning on it. We'd been talking for weeks after I met her at a school play. When I saw her leave the haunted house that day it was fate."

Zelda remained silent, staring at her lap. With a guttural moan, she started to push herself to standing. I dropped the phone and grabbed her, wrapping my arms around her and pulling her down next to me.

"Don't touch that, whore!" Nate screamed, spit flying. He sat forward on the sofa. The long, thin blade shook. I let my arms drop.

"You shut up," he commanded Zelda. She whimpered once and quieted. Light glinted off the blade.

"Why are you doing this?" I asked, my anger clear.

He smirked. "Why would I do this?" He laughed again. "Just this?" He moved the shiny blade back and forth in front of him. These games he played had my patience shot. "The short of it is I've been watching Zellie here for years. How many times did I ask you out?"

She rocked back and forth, her hair wiped from side to side, unable to answer.

"Let's just say it was a lot. She acted too good for me. Always. Too busy. Always with you." He spat the words.

"You killed people because she finally went out with you?"

He sunk into the cushions and crossed his legs. "All those years, I had to find things to keep me… occupied while I waited. I knew she would come to me. Only a matter of time."

I inhaled deeply and assessed the situation. We sat across from a madman with a viciously large knife. Zelda had mentally checked out. I had to catch him off guard to survive this. He would not get me. Not this time. Not again. Zelda and I would make it out of this.

He continued, "I dabbled in things. S and M, voyeurism, porn, line dancing. None of it felt as good as the wolf." He shivered. "When I became the wolf, it made me whole. I picked it up at a costume store that was going out of business. It wasn't long after that Zellie noticed me. Really noticed me. Remember that, babe?" He shivered again, the bitter smile widening.

Zelda stilled. She raised her head, her eyes grim and set. "The shaggy dog costume you wore all day on Halloween?"

His smile faltered.

"The one that smelled like ass?" Her tone strengthened. "The one that had bare patches and different color hair?"

Nate's smile fell.

Zelda straightened and reached for my hand. Her grip was steel. "The one all the students made fun of you when you wore it all day at school? That the one, Nate?"

"No!" Nate shouted, the word a missile. "You don't talk to me like that. Everyone loved it." His chest heaved. "That was the day I realized who I really was."

I racked my memory. A couple years ago the school staff celebrated holidays to the nines. Zelda dressed up as Poison Ivy, but everyone thought she was the Jolly Green Giant. For Christmas that year, she received several bags of frozen vegetables. But she looked cute. Nate's costume looked more like a thrift store Big Foot than a wolfman. He refused to take the costume off, which led to the administrators banning staff from dressing up.

"You wore this costume, got a hard on, and decided killing people was the way to go?" My voice rose in anger.

"You think you're so smart?" He shook his head. "It woke a part of me I didn't know existed. The authentic part of me. I am the wolf. That's who I am. My true nature."

Zelda opened her mouth, and I squeezed her hand. She got the signal and closed her mouth. Best to keep him distracted and not focused on her.

He continued, "I am the wolf. I fought the urge to hunt for so long. I did. But I gave in eventually. I had to, it overwhelmed me. It was all I could think about. I remember the first time like it was yesterday."

"Buffy?" I asked, trying to keep my voice calm.

His brows rose in surprise. "What? No." He shook

his head. "My first hunt was a year and three months ago. I was at a teaching convention in Baltimore and took the costume with me. I found hunting unfamiliar streets exhilarating." His chest rose, and he exhaled with a sigh. "The first one was dark curly hair, rich skin, bright eyes, thick, nice ass. I met her at the conference. No one ever knew it was me."

He just described Zelda exactly. "You've been killing people, then?" I regretted the words as soon as they left my mouth, but I had to say something to change the subject. Nate was deep in the delusion.

Nate tensed and held the knife tighter. "Hunting you mean. That's what I do. I hunt. Like a wild animal that can barely be contained. I am the untamed animal."

I remembered from my documentary binge-watching days wolves traveled in packs. "Did you do all of it with Dylan?"

The knife froze in Nate's hand. "What? No, no. He was a red herring. Easy to frame and the police here are too dumb to question it. I followed Buffy that day and couldn't resist any longer. When you started poking around, I was worried the police might think too hard and cleaned everything up."

"You are the one that broke in my house, killed Celeste then? All of it?"

He frowned. "You were always in the way, Lexi. If you would have just taken a hint and stayed away from Zelda…"

She squeezed my hand hard enough to hurt my fingers. "Am I responsible for this?"

Nate belly laughed. His face reddened. His laughter filled the room, sucking the air out. "It's just like you to think this is all about you, Zellie." His laughter died away with a sigh. "When we got together, when I finally had you, I thought I could stop hunting. You satisfied a certain… animalist need."

Her face reddened.

"But it wasn't enough. I wanted more, I had to have Buffy, so fresh, so…"

A knock at the door interrupted him.

Chapter Thirty-One

Nate's rabid gaze flashed to me. His knuckles whitened on the knife handle. "Who's at the door?"

"I'm not expecting anyone." My mind reeled, and I said a silent prayer that Shirley and Chester weren't on the other side of the door.

Nate stood in front of us, the gleam of the knife in my face. "Don't try anything." He yanked me to the door and mouthed for me to say something.

"Who is it?" I called out weakly.

"It's Scott. I forgot I had some of your stuff in my car." Low laughter filtered through the door. "Guess I was more focused on other things." Silence. "You okay?" His voice carried the smallest note of concern.

My muscles tensed at his tone. He sensed something was wrong. Most of the time the man couldn't figure out what I was trying to say but he came through when it was important. I didn't want him in this. Before I thought of anything to say, Nate shoved me aside and threw open the door. I caught myself on the entry table before hitting the ground. He grabbed Scott by the jacket and dragged him into the room. The door slammed shut behind them.

Nate held the knife to Scott's throat.

Scott's gaze slid around the room in one sweep and took in the situation. "Nate, man, what's going on?"

"Where's your gun?" The tip of the knife broke Scott's flesh.

"Look, it's at home, locked up." A drop of blood trickled down Scott's neck. "I don't carry it when I'm off duty. Pat me down. You'll see."

"It's true. I've never seen him carry a weapon unless he's on the clock," I interjected.

Nate's glare shifted between us, debating. "Fine, take a seat between them and don't try anything funny."

Zelda scooted to the end of the loveseat to make room for Scott. He squeezed in to join us. There would not be any sudden movements as close as we were. At least we weren't bound. We had a slim chance.

Nate took the same seat, crossing one leg over a knee. "Any who, where were we?" His gazed shifted to each of us. "Ah, yes," He frowned slightly. "My plan was to come here, kill you both and leave your bodies staged like the lesbos we all know you are."

I resisted the urge to roll my eyes. People had been saying that since before Zelda and I were what lesbians were. Folks usually gave us a hard time about our closeness. For the life of me, I never understood why it was their business. The fact that Nate brought it up now made him even crazier.

When the words didn't get a reaction, he continued. "But I'm bored with this."

"Haha," I laughed flatly. "Is that the reaction you want?"

Nate grimaced and his hand tightened on the knife handle. "But now I have this douche to consider." He pointed the knife at Scott. "You should have thrown her stuff in the trash. It's where she belongs anyway."

"You're right," Scott replied. "I shouldn't care. Like she didn't care for me." Hate oozed between each word. "They aren't worth the trouble."

Nate nodded. "You know it, man. These two are not worth the trouble. Look at this one." He gestured with the knife towards Zelda. "She doesn't respect me, tries to control everything. Spends all her time with this whore. Nothing but trash under my feet. All those years I fantasized about her, for what?"

Scott smiled. "Right, nothing but trash."

I understood Scott was attempting to build rapport with Nate, allowing his guard to come down. I once saw him do it at a festival. A drunk guy started causing trouble and Scott calmed him down to get the drunk on his side. This wasn't that simple. I had doubts Scott's strategy would work. Nate literally believed he was a wolf and currently held us captive with a large knife.

Nate stared at Scott for a long time before speaking. "You know what, man? We should kill them together. Have you ever taken a life before?" Nate licked his lips. "Best sensation ever."

A strangled moan escaped me. I might question Scott's work ethic but never his commitment to what was right before all of this. Now I easily saw him taking the side with this monster.

"It's been a long time," Scott answered. "I wouldn't mind getting my hands dirty again."

"Yes." Nate moved to the edge of the couch, waving the knife excitedly. "I always saw you were like me. Wild. An animal." He motioned with the knife to himself. "Inside."

"So what? You're just going to give up your morals and job and commit murder with this idiot?" Zelda asked, contempt in each word.

"Zelda…" I warned.

Scott shifted to glance at her. "What's to give up?

You don't think I can cover up a crime?" His laugh was harsh. "I've been around long enough I can do it in my sleep. Hell, I can make your murder look exactly like Nate here wants it to look. Murder suicide is my vote." He turned his gaze to Nate. "Which one you want, man?" He pointed a thumb at Zelda, eyebrows raised. "I'm guessing you've been waiting to do this one for awhile."

Nate's gaze moved between Zelda and me. "If only she would love me, like I love her. All of me and be with me. Just me," His features contorted. "But I had to share her and wolves don't share." He settled on Zelda for a moment before coming back to rest on me. Relief flooded through me. I wasn't strong enough to fight one of these men, much less two. But if it meant Zelda had a chance at getting out of here, I would do it.

"How about we do each other's bitch," he said. "I'll take Lexi. I haven't had the chance to really experience her life fully slipping away yet." The reach of the darkness in his eyes made my breath lock in my throat. "She's been a thorn in my side since the beginning. Always took Zelda away from me. I'll enjoy killing her this time."

Scott nodded and rubbed his hands down the legs of his jeans. "I'm going to enjoy this. You want me to use that, or you got another one?"

Nate held the knife out to Scott. "I brought just the one. But no rush. We can take our time. We got all night." The arousal was clear.

Scott moved to stand. "I'm going to enjoy this."

Zelda swung her arm around and with a cry that would have made Grandma Francis proud, she punched Scott square in the nuts.

Chapter Thirty-Two

Scott fell forward, clutched his groin, and landed face first on the floor. Knife forgotten to the side, Nate moved to him. Zelda barreled headfirst for Nate's midsection. I pushed myself over Scott on the floor and dove for the knife.

Nate and Zelda struggled on the couch. He was strong under the fluff, but she had weight and surprise on her side. My fingertips grazed the knife as Nate's hand slammed mine. I fought Nate's hand away and I reached for the knife again. He grasped at my face and pulled my hair. Pain shot through my scalp as his hand came away with a chunk. Zelda pummeled his midsection and groin with punches. Each one punctuated with a short scream. It didn't matter how much fighting I did, Nate's hand closed over the knife hilt. I sunk my teeth into his hand in a final effort.

"Stop moving." Scott's deadpan voice froze us in place.

I glanced over my shoulder. Scott stood with a gun trained on Nate. "Ladies, move." We didn't move but remained frozen in shock. "Now." The seriousness of his tone broke the moment.

Breathing heavily, we scramble across the floor against the furniture.

Scott threw handcuffs at Nate. "Drop the knife and cuff yourself."

Nate's now bloody hand tightened on the knife. His eyes were alight with madness. "And if I don't?"

"I don't want to shoot you, Nate."

Nate threw his hair over his shoulder. "You won't want to, but you will". The air hung thick between them for a breath before he lunged at Scott with the knife. "You lying sack of sh—"

The gunshot was deafening in the room. Gun powder strong. Nate fell back on the couch, his face contorted. I couldn't take my eyes off of him as he lay there, a large, spreading blossom of blood on his shirt.

My instincts and decades of experience kicked in. I stumbled to Nate and checked his pulse. It was there, but weak and thready. Scott grabbed the knife from Nate's hand and threw it as far away as possible. I ripped open Nate's shirt and examined the wound. Blood pumped out in a rhythmic flow. He had minutes, maybe seconds.

Behind us, Scott was on his cell, speaking in a low voice.

Nate's face grew more pale as the life drained from his eyes. I checked his pulse again and couldn't find it. The blood blossom slowed.

"He's dead?" Zelda asked quietly.

I nodded. Reaching a hand up, I closed his eyelids.

Zelda exhaled hard and nodded. "He was insane."

I pulled Zelda away from the scene and directed her to a seat at the kitchen island. My hands left bloody prints on her shoulders. "There's no words for what he was."

"Touch nothing or clean anything." Scott held a hand over the phone and said, "Just stay put."

I nodded, and we sat down. The blood drying on my skin, a familiar sensation and I pushed the panic down. "He was not right, that's for damn sure."

Her eyes were dry and wide, an expression of shock rather than sadness. She fell in love with a psycho and most definitely slept with one. This wasn't going to be easy. Her emotions would catch up later.

****

The next hours were filled with officers, ambulance staff, flashing lights, and soft voices. Since the shooting involved one of their own, the police department called in the Kansas City police to cover the investigation Nate's death. Appearances did matter after all.

Scott stayed in the living room, near where he fired the gun. Officers took our statements. They were kind and gave Zelda a bottle of water from the refrigerator. Scott was pale and clench-jawed as he answered questions.

Nate's blood stained the rug and the couch, drying to a deep crimson. Exhausted, my muscles ached, and my head hurt. Zelda leaned against me.

It would take us months, years to recover from this. The officers informed us they would need our clothes. We went upstairs to change with a female officer following and bagged the ones we were wearing. We still couldn't shower.

When we came downstairs, Scott was being led out between two uniformed officers.

"What's happening?" I asked, confused. Our statements were clear, it was self-defense.

"We're taking him to the Eastside precinct for processing, ma'am," a Kansas City officer said. "Then we'll bring him back here."

Scott shook his head. "No need. A friend is coming for my car."

"Your place then." They led Scott out the door and

down the front steps.

We were guided to dining chairs by another officer. He had taken our statements and had been kind, especially with Zelda once he heard it was her boyfriend that lay dead in the living room.

"Ladies, is there someplace else you can stay tonight? We need to finish processing the scene and it's going to take all night."

"We can stay at her house." I nodded towards Zelda.

His eyebrows raised. "You two don't live together?"

Zelda huffed. "No, I prefer things clean and organized. This one only cleans once an eclipse." Her voice was far away and detached.

The officer stared a moment longer and turned his attention to me. "Okay, I'll go upstairs with you and pack a bag. You need to head to her house." He motioned to Zelda. I nodded, and we headed upstairs. I packed a bag with a few changes of clothes, underwear, and a toothbrush. I didn't know how long I'd be gone but figured it would at least be a few days.

Before I left, I texted Shirley and Chester a shorter version of what happened. They didn't reply but came flying across the lawn to meet up in the driveway. Taking in Zelda's vacant stare, they stopped short.

Shirley grasped her shoulder. "Honey, you okay?" When there was no response, Shirley gave her a hard shake and asked again.

"Shirl…" Chester started, standing behind her.

The sob erupted deep in Zelda and broke out in a wail that froze my heart. Shirley caught Zelda as she collapsed in her arms. Chester and I rushed in as they sunk in the grass. Shirley had Zelda enveloped in her meaty arms, rocking her back and forth. I knelt down next to them. Chester squatted down on the other side. My throat was tightened. Nate had been unhinged, and I had little doubt he wouldn't hurt Chester and Shirley if he felt they were in his way. We were lucky to have gotten through this night.

The police gave us a wide berth, circling us in the driveway. We stayed like that for a long time until Zelda's moaning dissolved into soft cries.

"There, there, baby." Shirley cooed in Zelda's hair. "We gotta get you out of this cold. Let's get you into the car." She patted Zelda's back and rubbed her hands up and down her arms.

Zelda's head bobbed and she sniffed loudly, wiping her hand across her nose. "I thought you all were dead."

Chester stood and lifted Zelda with him and clicked his tongue. "It's gonna take more than a filthy beast to do us in." He helped Shirley up and then directed us all to my car. "Let us get you out of here."

Chapter Thirty-Three

It was a slow drive to Zelda's house. I hadn't been behind the wheel in months, but traffic was thankfully nonexistent at this hour. My whole body was sore by the time we unloaded in her carport next to the house.

I directed her to the bathroom, and shuffled to the guest bathroom and started the shower, letting the water steam up the room before I got in. Once under the water, the recent events overwhelmed me. Tears flowed, and I wept for everything that happened. Celeste didn't need to die. Buffy was innocent of everything. Even Dylan, who wasn't the purest soul, didn't deserve his ending. I stayed under the water until it ran cold. Dressed in one of my pioneer nightgowns, I tiptoed into Zelda's bedroom to check on her.

The snores carried through the closed door. She was wrapped in blankets and fluffy comforters with only the top of her hair poking out. On the nightstand sat a bottle of muscle relaxants and a small glass of water, half empty. I reached between the blankets to her neck, checking her pulse. It was steady and strong. Even so, I took the bottle of meds and closed the door behind me. There had been enough death; I didn't want an accidental one tonight.

In the guest room, I tucked the bottle in the nightstand and snuggled under the blankets, savoring the warmth. I drifted off to sleep, wondering why I still felt numb after all the tears. My sleep was disjointed, and I tossed and turned, unable to wake up from the disturbing dreams.

I was lying in bed late the next morning trying to make sense of all the recent events when my cell phone pinged a notification from Chief Wagner.

—*Good morning, Lexi. Are you ready to talk for a bit?*—

—*Yes, I'm at Zelda's. Still in bed. Give me 30 minutes.*—

—*No problem. I'm at the bakery on Main and will bring something.*—

My stomach grumbled. I threw clothes on before heading down the hall. Outside of Zelda's room, I put my ear against the door and listened for any sign of movement. Sounds of Zelda's chainsaw snoring vibrated. I debated about waking her but thought better of it. She needed to rest.

I poked around the spotless kitchen and was making coffee when my phone texted again. It was the Chief.

—*I'm outside.*—

I hurried to the front door to open it, but my hand froze on the doorknob. My breath caught in my chest and the blood puddled to my feet. "You're being ridiculous, Lex," I said to myself as I gripped the knob tight and plastered a smile on my face.

I opened the door to Chief Wagner in faded jeans and a worn Atherton High School sweatshirt. He had a large, grease-stained bag and a tray of coffee cups in his hands.

"I assume you still can't make coffee?" he asked, referring to an incident in high school where I put a half a can of coffee grounds in the filter in the sports office.

Those coaches didn't know what hit them. Over the years, my coffee making had improved but not by much.

I held the door open and motioned him inside. "I have learned a few things." I sniffed as he walked by and caught a whiff of fat and sugar. "But if there's a mocha in one of those cups, you will have my undying gratitude."

"Then I will go to my grave a happy man with the gratitude of a good woman."

My eyebrows raised at his comment. I guess his attitude of me just wiping butts for a living had changed. He sat the items down on the table and handed me a cup. I sipped the warm, gooey coffee and it warmed my throat and stomach.

He sat down at the table and took a cup. "How are you doing this morning? Unofficially."

I wrapped my hands around the cup. "I'm okay. Sore. Tired." I shrugged. "But what's new?"

"To be expected," he said, poking a finger at the bag of sweets. "And Zelda? She okay?"

"I haven't wakened her yet. Figured I'd let her sleep."

He held the bag out to me, and I grabbed a glazed donut and a chocolate one with sprinkles. He nodded. "Probably for the best. That lady has it rough. You both do. Heard you resigned from the hospital." He grabbed a donut too and chewed, letting his words hang between us.

"Yeah, I need a change, something different." The crunchy sugar coating of the donut was heaven with the still warm inside.

"You okay, got some money put back?" This was the fatherly old friend I wanted to remember, not the hard-bitten cop.

"There's enough in savings to explore my next move."

He nodded and wiped icing from his mouth with the back of his hand. "Good, with everything you've been through... I want to make sure you were doing it for the right reasons."

My eyes misted over. "Thanks, Chief. I appreciate it, I just need to do something different. Isn't that what the Gen-X's all do? Have a career or two? I have to catch up." I faked a laugh and covered my face with the coffee mug.

He shook his head. "I don't know anything about that, but I trust you to do what's best. You can always call me if you need anything. Hell, I even have a position open. Nakamura's son was the worst damn desk jockey I've ever had. If you're interested."

I laughed. It wouldn't take long for the police force to take bets on who was worse, me or Nakamura. "I'll pass on that. And keep you in mind if I need anything."

"Well, I won't be around much after next fall." His face scrunched up, giving his features the appearance of a gnarly tree knot. "Going to finally retire, buy an RV and see the country."

I nodded. That didn't sound like a bad idea. The open road, quiet evenings by starlight. I loved Zelda but being in that close quarters could drive one of us to murder. "What did you want to talk about?"

He wiped his hands together to free them of powdered sugar. "I read the reports the officers took last night and just wanted to check on you both. Are you really all right?"

I shrugged and shoved a donut in my mouth. Every

time someone asked me, I declared loudly I was fine and doing okay. I wasn't so sure anymore.

The Chief respected my silence and continued to sit with me, enjoying bites of donuts and coffee. After I finished my donuts, I sighed and wiped the sugar off my hands.

"Honestly, I think I'm fine. We'll be fine, Zelda and me. Might have a few moments here and there."

He leaned back in the chair, his fingers drummed on the table. "Gotta say something about that boy always rubbed me wrong. Thought it was the hair." The Chief waved his hands around his shoulders. "I never thought he had done something like this. And he did it good. Most people that try to frame someone else do a shitty job of it. Take Scott. He's a good cop but if he had tried, he would have screwed it up three different ways. I have a theory the good, smart ones think too hard and foul themselves up."

"At least the ones that get caught," I added.

His eyebrows raised, and he nodded. "True. Although I don't like to contemplate the ones that don't. They might not even be on our radar. I like to hold we have a law-abiding town full of good people."

"Recent events make me question that. Do you consider yourself part of the good people?" I reached out on a limb with the question, but I couldn't miss the opportunity. I wasn't sure who the good people were.

When he finally spoke, his voice was quiet. "Generally speaking, I do. But sometimes I have to make hard decisions. One's I don't like, but someone has to make them." He threw up his hands in defeat. "It is what it is."

I grabbed another donut and tore a piece off and

chewed thoughtfully. "I didn't realize how many decisions you make that are in the gray area."

He nodded. "Life isn't black and white. Hell, most of the time it's barely gray." He took a sip of coffee. "Well... I should be headed out."

"Did you want to talk to Zelda?"

He stood, hitching up the jeans over slim hips. "Nope, like I said, here unofficially. Checking on you two. Boys got all we needed last night. Can't afford for the town to lose two upstanding citizens like yourselves," he said with a wink before closing the door behind himself.

I stared at the door and thought about our conversation. We had many unknowns ahead of us but I knew with good people around us we'd come out okay.

"Was that the Chief?" Zelda asked, groggy and hair standing out in all directions. She dropped into the chair across from me and immediately clawed into the bag of donuts.

I pushed a coffee towards her. "Yep. He wanted to check on us." I took in her wrinkled face and hair everywhere. "How are you?"

She took the cup and chugged. "Eh? I've been better, that's for damn sure. I can't even imagine how much sage it's going to take to cleanse this situation."

"We'll need something more legitimate than sage, perhaps therapy?"

She fished a chocolate croissant out of the bag and rolled her eyes. "Why would I ever need therapy? It's not every day the guy you're dating turns out to be a serial killer who gets off on wearing a stinky ass werewolf costume." She tore the pastry and shoved a junk in her mouth. "Perfectly fucking normal. Who wouldn't be great?"

Her sarcasm made me smile. One might beat Zelda down, but she'd always get back up. I sipped my coffee and watched her down coffee and pastries. Zelda's exterior was harder than cement, but her soul was gentle as a baby's.

She swallowed and shrugged. "I will have to go to therapy. And lots of it." She popped half an almond croissant in her mouth. "Probably overdue."

"Honestly, after some of the other men you've dated, I'm surprised you haven't gone yet, either."

Zelda blew a raspberry at me before taking a loud sip of coffee. "You're not wrong." She drummed the cup on the table. "I haven't done well with men. And will make sure that's covered in first. In all seriousness, we both have a way to go on recovering from all of this."

"I agree with that." I raised my almost empty cup in salute.

"How about for right now, can we just live and enjoy life?"

A filthy murderer couldn't kill Zelda or my will to live. I smiled and she raised her coffee cup to toast mine. "To living and enjoying life." The paper cups made no sound when they touched. "To Hawaii or wherever adventures may take us on."

Zelda returned my smile, and the sparkle back to her eyes. "Amen to that, sister."

A word about the author...

Emily Karmazin, a long time fan of snacks and 80's television, currently lives in the Wasatch Mountains of Utah with her husband and their dogs. She wrote her first book in third grade, a fanfic of Little House on the Prairie. She has an interest in travel, reading, learning new things, hiking, all things strange and usual, and baking. ekarmazin18.wixsite.com/mysite

Thank you for purchasing
this publication of The Wild Rose Press, Inc.

For questions or more information
contact us at
info@thewildrosepress.com.

The Wild Rose Press, Inc.
www.thewildrosepress.com